CRIME SCENE INVESTIGATIONS

Cybercrime

Using Computers as Weapons

By Mike Sciandra

Portions of this book originally appeared in *Cybercrime* by Kevin Hile.

LUCENT PRESS

Published in 2018 by
Lucent Press, an Imprint of Greenhaven Publishing, LLC
353 3rd Avenue
Suite 255
New York, NY 10010

Designer: Deanna Paternostro
Editor: Siyavush Saidian

Library of Congress Cataloging-in-Publication Data

Names: Sciandra, Mike.
Title: Cybercrime: using computers as weapons / Mike Sciandra.
Description: New York : Lucent Press, 2018. | Series: Crime scene investigations | Includes index.
Identifiers: ISBN 9781534560918 (library bound) | ISBN 9781534560925 (ebook)
Subjects: LCSH: Computer crimes–Juvenile literature.
Classification: LCC HV6773.H55 2018 | DDC 364.16'8–dc23

Printed in the United States of America

CPSIA compliance information: Batch #BS17KL: For further information contact Greenhaven Publishing LLC, New York, New York at 1-844-317-7404.

Please visit our website, www.greenhavenpublishing.com. For a free color catalog of all our high-quality books, call toll free 1-844-317-7404 or fax 1-844-317-7405.

Contents

Foreword

For decades, popular television programs and movies have depicted the life and work of police officers, detectives, and crime scene investigators. Most of these shows and films portray forensic scientists as the brains responsible for cracking cases and bringing criminals to justice. Undoubtedly, these crime scene analysts are an important part in the process of crime solving. With modern technology and advances in forensic analysis, these highly trained experts play a crucial component of law enforcement systems all across the world.

Police officers and detectives are also integral members of the law enforcement team. They are the ones who respond to 911 calls about crime, collect physical evidence, and use their high level of training to identify suspects and culprits. They work right alongside forensic investigators to figure out the mysteries behind why a crime is committed, and the entire team cooperates to gather enough evidence to convict someone in a court of law.

Ever since the first laws were recorded, crime scene investigation has been handled in roughly the same way. An authority is informed that a crime has been committed; someone looks around the crime scene and interviews potential witnesses; suspects are identified based on evidence and testimony; and, finally, someone is formally accused of committing a crime. This basic plan is generally effective, and criminals are often caught and brought to justice. Throughout history, however, certain limitations have sometimes prevented authorities from finding out who was responsible for a crime.

There are many reasons why a crime goes unsolved: Maybe a dead body was found too late, evidence was tampered with, or witnesses lied. Sometimes, even the greatest technology of the age is simply not good enough to process and analyze the evidence at a crime scene. In the United States during the 20th century, for example, the person responsible for the infamous Zodiac killings was never found, despite the earnest efforts of hundreds of policemen, detectives, and forensic analysts.

In modern times, science and technology are integral to the investigative process. From DNA analysis to high-definition surveillance video, it has become much more difficult to commit a crime and get away with it. Using advanced computers and immense databases, microscopic skin cells from a crime scene can be collected and then analyzed by a forensic scientist, leading detectives to the home of the culprit of a crime. Dozens of people work behind the scenes of criminal investigations to figure out the unique and complex elements of a crime. Although this process is still time-consuming and complicated, technology is constantly improving and adapting to the needs of police forces worldwide.

This series is designed to help young readers understand the systems in place to allow forensic professionals to do their jobs. Covering a wide range of topics, from the assassination of President John F. Kennedy to 21st-century cybercriminals, these titles describe in detail the ways in which technology and criminal investigations have evolved over more than 50 years. They cite eyewitnesses and experts in order to give a detailed and nuanced picture of the difficult task of rooting out criminals. Although television shows and movies add drama to the crime scene investigation process, these real-life stories have enough drama on their own. This series sticks to the facts surrounding some of the highest-profile criminal cases of the modern era and the people who work to solve them and other crimes every day.

Introduction

A New Age of Computer Technology

When computers and the Internet first came into common use in the 1980s and 1990s, they were hailed as ushering in a new era of efficient, paperless offices. Their use expanded rapidly and they would soon become a new platform for free speech through the World Wide Web. That freedom of communication and secure electronic storage of data has unquestionably improved the lives of billions of people. However, it has also come under attack by criminals who have learned to use the Internet for everything from personal gain to computer data vandalism.

Today, a great deal of time, effort, and money is being spent by computer users, both professionally and at home, to protect themselves from these threats. Most people who use computers are now aware of the need to install security software, such as antivirus protection and firewalls. These programs require frequent updating and monitoring and must be run regularly to effectively keep computers safe. Many people are also aware of the hazards of suspicious e-mail messages that are made to look innocent while hiding malicious software that may wipe out the memory on a hard drive or steal personal information.

How Cybercrime Has Evolved

News reports of widespread threats to computer safety have become increasingly common since the turn of the 21st century. In one of the earlier instances on July 30, 2008, the Federal Bureau of Investigation (FBI) issued an alert for people to watch out for the Storm Worm spam e-mail. The message appeared to offer information about the social networking website Facebook as well as the FBI, but when users clicked a link in the text, a website would open and upload

In the 21st century, physical crime scenes identified by tape and flashing lights are often exchanged for a desktop computer.

The law enforcement officers who investigate cybercrime have to find complex digital clues.

a computer worm onto their hard drive. This virus made the victims' computers "zombies," meaning they were taken over by a remote master computer that could control their operation.

While computer viruses and spam e-mails are what generally spring to mind when people think about computer crime, almost any type of crime can be aided with the use of technology—including everything from identity theft to sexual harassment to hate crime. Police and federal law enforcement agencies have been struggling to keep up with this growing trend using the increasingly important field of computer forensics to battle these cyber criminals. It is still difficult, though, for the average person to be sure who the bad guys are and who the good guys are, because cybercrooks have mastered the ability to disguise themselves as other people, companies, and even law enforcement.

Computer forensics can go a long way in unraveling the complex digital clues that cybercriminals leave behind. The study of forensic computer science combines fields that have become exciting for young people considering a career in law enforcement: information technology and traditional crime-scene investigation methods. The study of forensics, however, is not for everyone. It takes years of training, discipline, and technical know-how; but for those who are up to the challenge, it can be a rewarding and profitable career choice. Computer forensic experts are in high demand for the foreseeable future as criminals and high-end technology become more advanced.

Chapter One
Defining Cybercrime

When a resource is made available to the public with the potential to both help and harm humankind, there are always people who will twist the capabilities of that resource to cause harm. The popularization of computer technology is no exception. Because cybercrime is on the cutting edge of law enforcement, police, federal agents, and the legal system are constantly being challenged by unexpected uses of this technology. People who fight cybercrime almost always rely on computer forensics to track down perpetrators.

The word cybercrime is a general term for many types of criminal behavior involving computers and other types of high-tech equipment. The "cyber-" in the word comes from the word cyberspace, which was popularized by author William Gibson in his 1984 science-fiction novel *Neuromancer*. Gibson wrote about a virtual world that existed within computers and computer networks. Cybercrime, accordingly, refers to crimes that are perpetrated using computer technology and happen primarily in cyberspace. In the past, and in some rare instances today, such crimes were performed on-site, such as on a computer located at a business. In the 21st century, however, lawbreakers more commonly use the Internet from remote locations for illegal activities.

The Enemy with No Face

In the last few months of 2016, the U.S. Army's "Cyber" commercial aired, running frequently on major networks and in ads before YouTube videos. The commercial showed a single laptop computer on a desk in a seemingly abandoned room, with nobody in front of it. As the camera zoomed in, keyboard clicks sounded off as white text appeared on the black screen and a disguised voice spoke. "I can shut down your power grids," it said. "And I can paralyze your infrastructure. I can access the personal data of everyone in America. I am the enemy with no face, and I can't be—."[1] The word "stopped" was interrupted and the commercial cut to a room full of U.S. Army personnel on computers, taking on the threat.

One unique characteristic of cybercrime and a key advantage to such criminals exemplified in commercials like this is the power of anonymity. Before advanced computer networks and the Internet came into existence, most crimes were committed in person. A notable exception is mail fraud, or using letters or other items sent through the postal service to commit crimes that commonly involve personal information theft. Today, however, cybercriminals can steal, scam, destroy information, and hurt people in other ways without the victims ever seeing them or knowing their identity.

A dangerous result is that potential criminals feel less danger because they can hide behind a screen. With their identities hidden, people who otherwise might not commit a crime are more tempted to do so. Internet anonymity makes tracking criminals a bigger challenge for investigators because lawbreakers are constantly finding new ways to prevent law enforcement agencies from locating them.

Cyberbullying has been on the rise as more youths are accessing social media websites, where much cyberbullying occurs.

Bullies, Vigilantes, Terrorists

Cyberbullying is a broad topic. It can be anything, such as a thread of hurtful comments on a Facebook post, a specific message, or an e-mail directly from one user to another. Cyberbullies can be on the other side of the world, or peers from school sharing an embarrassing photo to harass someone online. In Pennsylvania in 2006, before the state created any law against cyberbullying, a group of teenagers set up a MySpace profile about a 16-year-old girl including a lot of malicious gossip and photographs that had been digitally altered to embarrass her. In other cases, both across America and across the globe, there have been cases of cyberbullying in which the victim, terrorized online, has taken their own life.

Cybervigilantes, sometimes called "hacktivists" are people who use the Internet to seek justice against people they believe are criminals. Cybervigilantes often make these people's names public—on blogs, in chat rooms, and in message boards—without going through the process of law. A worldwide vigilante group named Anonymous has made frequent examples of its skill online since 2008, when it gained access into the Church of Scientology website with a distributed denial of service (DDoS) attack, in which multiple computers flooded the website with requests to the point of a network shutdown.

Cyberterrorists use the Internet to promote a terrorist agenda or commit acts of terror, often intending to damage or disrupt computer systems and compromise enemies. This type of terrorist, often revealed as both foreign and domestic hackers, steal data, flood networks with data until they crash, and attack digitally maintained infrastructure for various purposes. Ardit Ferizi, a hacker from Kosovo who provided the terrorist group ISIS with more than 1,000 names of U.S. government and military personnel, was the first person in the United States convicted of both computer hacking and terrorism charges. He was sentenced to 20 years in prison in 2016.

Another difficulty with cybercrime is that incidents can be so cutting-edge that the legal system has not created laws against them. Thus, the activities cannot be prosecuted as crimes. For example, though cyberbullying (harassing people—frequently teens or young adults—over the Internet, by e-mail, on social media or other websites) has made national headlines in the 2010s, only 48 American states have some form of regulation against it and there are no federal laws as of 2017.

The Different Types of Cybercriminals

David S. Wall, professor of criminology at the University of Leeds in England, has categorized computer crimes into three types: computer-integrity

Members of Anonymous are associated with masks similar to this, which are made in the image of a 16th century revolutionary from England.

crimes, computer-assisted crimes, and computer-content crimes. In his book, *Cybercrime: The Transformation of Crime in the Information Age*, Wall explained that computer-integrity crimes "include hacking and cracking, vandalism, spying, denial of service, the planting and use of viruses and Trojans."[2] Wall also wrote, "Computer-assisted crimes use networked computers to commit crimes, usually to acquire money, goods or services dishonestly,"[3] and that computer-content crimes " are related to the illegal content on networked computer systems and include the trade and distribution of [sexual] materials as well as the dissemination [spread] of hate crime materials."[4]

Within these categories, one of the most common types of cybercrime is creating or spreading a computer virus. Viruses are small programs that invade a computer's hard drive. They have various specific functions, but generally they deliberately damage the computer, make it impossible to use, or even to steal information that is on the hard drive. Related to viruses are Trojans, programs that create secret passages to a computer, which allows other unwanted or aggressive programs to enter. This is how Trojans also allow criminals to more easily attack a computer. Another variety, called worms, are programs that reproduce themselves within a computer to spread through a computer network or through the Internet. Together, viruses, Trojans, and worms are called malicious software, or malware.

When someone mentions illegal computer activity, malware is among the first things that come to mind. However, there are many other ways that criminals can use technology to do damage, steal money, and ruin lives. Among these are sending spam e-mails, posting

Malware is the most common weapon cybercriminals employ to compromise computers, phones, networks, and other devices.

messages on social media platforms, luring people into business scams, and other illegal activities. This method of enticing computer users into a trap is called social engineering. By pretending to be a potential friend or business partner, criminals can lead their victims into illegal business scams, dangerous websites, and false advertisements.

In addition to damaging property and stealing information, cybercriminals can modify and falsify data to their own advantage. This is called data diddling, and it is an old practice. In one case from the late 1960s, corporate leaders at the investment company Equity Funding Corporation of America devised a plan to offer investors the opportunity to buy insurance policies and mutual funds at the same time. At first, they were highly successful, but when their actual profits did not match the predictions they were providing to investors, the company deliberately changed the information in their computer database. They created fictional sales of insurance policies at an unbelievably high rate. The *Computer Security Handbook* described the fraud: "By late 1972, the head of [data processing] calculated that by the end of the decade, at this rate, Equity Funding would have insured the entire population of the world. Its assets would surpass the gross national product of the planet. The president [of the company] merely insisted that this showed how well the company was doing."[5] In 1972, a disgruntled Equity Funding employee reported the fraud to the U.S. Securities and Exchange Commission (SEC), a government agency established to protect investors from unfair trade and market practices. After an investigation, the company's executives were arrested.

In the Equity Funding case, the illegal actions were actually encouraged by the company's officers. However, in some cases of corporate data diddling, employees can act independently, changing or destroying corporate data in acts of revenge against their employers. A typical example is when an employee is fired from their job and attempts to steal or destroy company property. To prevent this, companies will often deny an employee access to computers just before firing them.

Zombie Computers

When a backdoor is created by something like a Trojan, even the most well-protected computer can be converted into a "zombie." Zombie is a name for a computer taken over by a malicious program to spread more viruses and worms throughout a network of connected devices. Though they are named zombies, the affected computers are also similar to robots, because they obey their new programming. A network of infected zombie computers is often referred to as a botnet, a shortening of "robot network."

Trojans and botnets can combine to carry out a distributed denial of service (DDoS) attack on any network in the world. When a DDoS attack is sent out over the Internet, it targets computer servers, making requests for website pages to be accessed. It makes so many requests so rapidly that the server cannot handle the load and it eventually crashes. One famous DDoS attack, known as the Mirai virus, appeared in late 2016. The worm took over millions of Internet addresses and nearly 500,000 devices in the first month of its existence. The Mirai botnet is one of the largest ever, as it used millions of systems to create one of the largest DDoS attacks in cybercrime history. Though the source code was eventually released and security experts constructed defenses against it, the Mirai virus remained difficult to contain by even the foremost experts in cybersecurity.

Viruses and other malware are frequently distributed by spam, or unsolicited e-mails. Spam can also be used to prompt e-mail recipients to click on

Significant damage is often done by the time a computer's virus protection software detects a virus.

a link to a website that asks the visitor to input personal information. Such websites can be cleverly designed to appear like legitimate websites, such as those run by banks, financial advisers, and credit card companies. When people enter sensitive data, such as their Social Security number, into websites run by cybercriminals, they can find themselves the victim of online identity theft.

Malware can also infect Internet servers by going through social media websites, message boards, and discussion groups. The 1999 Melissa virus, for example, was first spread by users who visited a discussion group, where people thought they were getting free access to websites that required a password by downloading a list of stolen login information. Once these initial users downloaded the virus, however, it attacked their computers and quickly spread through e-mails.

By the Numbers

1 million

estimated number of cyberattacks per day

Hackers on Both Sides

Even before the Internet became a widespread phenomenon, cybercriminals could access information on a stand-alone computer and steal important data. This was the type of crime that began to trouble businesses during the early days of the technological revolution.

When computers first began to be used, a considerable number of those breaking into computer databases and the first networks did so because they wanted to prove their programming skills. In essence, they wanted to show off what they could do to their fellow programmers—and potential employers. Sometimes, too, hacking into computers was done to test network and database security. Corporations, lawyers, and others hire skilled hackers, nicknamed "samurai," to conduct legal computer surveillance, serve as advisers in court cases, or help businesses and law agencies access systems for legal investigative purposes. Samurai also test computer systems for potential vulnerabilities.

Such hackers—also sometimes called "white hats" because they typically work within the law—still exist today. Often, they are appreciated and even utilized by law enforcement, but some hackers who see themselves as the good guys are still regarded as criminals. In 2016, for example, the largest data leak in history occurred when a

How Viruses Infect Computers

Modern cybercriminals use programs, such as viruses, to access computers remotely far more often than directly. In the early days of computing, however, viruses were passed from computer to computer through floppy discs. Unsuspecting users would receive a computer disc from a friend or colleague, insert it into a drive, and the virus would download as soon as the disc was accessed. Viruses are mostly executable files (they almost always have ".exe" file extensions), meaning they must be accessed or run, often by opening a file or clicking a link. Today, these viruses are spread primarily through e-mail, websites, and other digital channels.

While many viruses damage data on a computer, some of the first viruses were written by programmers and academics who did not intend to cause any mischief. The Brain virus was written by two brothers: Basit and Amjad Farooq Alvi, who created a program that left their calling card (a file containing text that identified them, their phone number, and the address of their computer store in Pakistan) on people's computers. They wrote the virus not to destroy data, but to see where their business address ended up—and pinpoint computers that were downloading their software illegally.

Computer worms, while similar to viruses, can spread by themselves because they spread through network connections rather than through e-mails or file sharing. The Morris worm, which was one of the first worms, was written in 1988 by Robert Morris, a student at Cornell University. Morris created the program to study how such programs spread and gauge the current size of the Internet—but he wrote some incorrect code by mistake. The virus ended up spreading throughout the Internet, making thousands of computers inoperable.

Other famous viruses include the ILOVEYOU virus, which was distributed by e-mail in 2000. The virus sent out an e-mail with subject line "I Love You," prompting the unsuspecting recipient to open the e-mail. Once opened, the virus downloaded onto the computer, destroyed data (especially media files),stole e-mails, and replicated itself so it could spread to other computers. It caused an estimated $15 billion of damages worldwide. Even this vast amount pales in comparison to what was probably the most destructive malware of all time: MyDoom, unleashed onto global computers in the early 2000s. It caused huge DDoS attacks on some of the most powerful technology companies in the world, including Microsoft and Google, and infected millions of e-mails. Experts have estimated that it caused $38 billion worth of damages.

One of the most popular forms of viruses, Trojans are named after the Trojan horse of mythology. In the ancient Greek myth, the Achaeans tricked the citizens of Troy

hacker or group of hackers leaked more than 11 million documents from an offshore law firm. These leaked files, which exposed the finances of some of the world's most powerful people, were named the Panama Papers. After being into letting them inside the city walls by presenting the gift of a large wooden horse. When the Trojans pulled the horse inside their gates, enemy soldiers hidden inside the horse broke out and attacked. Accordingly, Trojan malware programs work in a similar fashion: They appear to be legitimate programs or files provided by someone known to the computer user. Trojans, unlike viruses or worms, do not replicate themselves. Once opened, however, they can cause serious damage to a computer, and they create a backdoor program that allows a criminal to then more easily access the computer's files.

Viruses were once passed around through e-mails, but recent innovations by cybercriminals have allowed viruses to download themselves onto most devices in other ways.

leaked to European news agencies by anonymous hacktivists, people around the world were outraged to learn of the billions of dollars held in offshore accounts—meaning they were largely untaxed—held by Russian president

Vladimir Putin, former British prime minister David Cameron, and hundreds of other wealthy and powerful individuals. Despite public support for this information being leaked, the hackers responsible were still cybercriminals.

Modern cybercrime, including large data breaches, such as the Panama Papers, and small e-mail viruses, grew out of the late–20th century push toward advanced computing. In the early years, it was much more difficult to break into a computer system, and those who could do so were admired by other programmers. The best hackers were proclaimed to be "gurus" or "wizards." Often, the wizards who offered to explain a system's weakness to a software company were offered jobs. However, when white hats turned to criminal activities and worked directly against the law, they were called "crackers" or "black hats."

Over time, the programs written by these skilled people made their way onto the Internet through message boards, chat rooms, and websites. It became easier to find samples of computer coding that could be copied and then used to hack into databases and servers without being well versed in writing code. People who are unskilled in programming and find and reuse code are often referred

The annual Black Hat convention is where the most cutting-edge discussions on cybersecurity and cybercrime take place.

One Young Hacker

Arriving with the new millennium were newly capable computer wizards and gurus who would set the standard for necessary cybersecurity in the 21st century, and their extremely young ages would surprise everyone.

In 2000, Jonathan James was the first minor to serve time for cybercrime—he was 16 years old when he was sentenced to six months in juvenile detention. James, who went by the alias "C0mrade," pleaded guilty to juvenile delinquency for repeatedly breaking into the networks of the Pentagon and NASA, where he specifically caused a 21-day shutdown of the computers supporting the international space station in 1999. While in the NASA system, he downloaded the software used for the International Space Station. The break-in caused NASA to shut down the system, and repairs cost more than $40,000. His father, Robert James, is a computer analyst, and he revealed his son's name to the public and defended his actions. Robert claimed that Jonathan's skills far surpassed his own, and insisted that his son's hacking had no seriously negative consequences.

In 2008, Jonathan James took his own life for fear of conviction for computer crimes he had not committed. While James's story ended tragically, a generation of young hackers with skills far beyond that of their predecessors was already on the horizon, and his actions called attention to both the current inadequacies of cybercrime investigations as well as the challenges of addressing mental health concerns in teenagers.

to as "script kiddies," which is an insult.

Today, a large social community has evolved around hackers and computer security in general. There are even hacker conferences, such as DEF CON, HOPE, and the Black Hat convention, and both online and print publications, such as *2600 Magazine*.

The Age of Cyberterrorism

Like the direct relationship between technological advances and cybercrime, when government and infrastructure rely on technology, they become vulnerable to a new form of attack. The term "cyberterrorism" was coined in the 1980s by Barry Collin, a senior research fellow from the Institute for Security and Intelligence in California. He defined it as "the convergence of cybernetics and terrorism."[6] The definition has evolved several times since then, and in 2011, the Center for Strategic and International Studies defined it as "the use of computer network tools to shut down critical national infrastructures (e.g., energy, transportation, government operations) or to coerce or intimidate a government or civilian population."[7]

Similarly to how the exact definition has seen changes, cyberterrorism can take many forms. It could be an attack on vital infrastructure, such as power grids and hospital networks, an attack on data storage or secure information, such as bank accounts, or even an attack on national security, such as the illegal spread of classified information or flooding a government network with data. Widespread action alone does not necessarily define cyberterrorism, but any data breach by a known terrorist organization may also be considered cyberterrorism if it promotes a political agenda or targets a specific group.

The first definitive cyberterrorism conviction in the United States took place in 2016, when 20-year-old Ardit Ferizi was sentenced to 20 years in prison for hacking into the server of a U.S. company to steal the personal information, including names, of more than 1,000 U.S. military members and government workers for the ISIS terrorist group. Ferizi, who went by the alias "Th3Dir3ctorY", was alleged to be the leader of Kosova Hacker's Security, a hacking group based in Kosovo, and his attacks were a crucial reminder that international cybersecurity still has to compete with the advancing intellects of young hackers.

Although Ferizi's case represented the first U.S. cyberterrorism conviction and an example of a foreign hacker, one of the first documented cyberterrorist attacks came in 1996 when an anonymous hacker, believed to be associated with the racist white supremacist movement, took down a Massachusetts Internet service provider (ISP) and damaged a portion of its records when the company attempted to stop them from circulating racist messages. If computer forensics were as sophisticated in the 1990s as they are now, this hacker could have been caught like Ferizi was. It is unquestionable that cyberterrorism, both in the United States and in countless other nations with advanced technology around the world, has both foreign and domestic enemies.

The Costs of Crime, Terror, and Espionage

The price of any variety of cybercrime runs high, whether financial, social, or personal. Some have argued that the laws regarding cybercrime in the United States—which are constantly shifting and changing—are too severe. For example, thousands of people voiced disgust when Matthew Keys was sentenced to two years in prison in 2016 after he allowed Anonymous to hack into his former employer's computers. Keys's supporters said that the only thing that happened because of the breach was an altered headline in the

Los Angeles Times, which they claimed was not enough to justify a two-year sentence. Conversely, Aleksandr Panin and Hamza Bendelladj were sentenced to a combined 24 years and 6 months in prison in 2016. They were convicted of creating and spreading a destructive virus, named SpyEye, which caused nearly $1 billion in damages across the world.

SpyEye was a kind of Internet fraud, which has become the most common type of cybercrime. Powerful criminal groups, such as the Mafia, have gotten involved; for example, organized criminals have set up gambling websites that are based overseas, to avoid American regulations and taxes, but easily accessed anywhere in the world. Gamblers who play on these dangerous websites quickly find themselves losing money and having their credit card information stolen while they play.

Another venue for computer fraud is the online auction. Popular websites, such as eBay, can be a home for unscrupulous dealers who offer goods at auction. Once someone wins an auction and sends money to the seller, the buyer either does not receive the correct item or does not receive anything at all. Auctioning companies similar to eBay try hard to block such scammers from their websites, but some websites have become so large that patrolling them is challenging and, thus, some criminals go unchecked.

On an international level, the Internet also has become a useful tool for both thieves and criminals who profit by sharing private or sensitive information. In 2017, the United States put 2 criminal hackers and 2 Russian spies on trial for breaching Yahoo's data servers and exposing 500 million e-mail and personal accounts. According to court filings against the men, they were paid by Russian officials to break into Yahoo and give the Russian government information about international political figures and businesspeople. The trial is expected to take several years to reach a conclusion.

Cyberextortion

On a smaller scale of cybercrime, but still damaging, is cyberextortion. While online bullies attack individuals to cause personal embarrassment and cyberterrorists attack to advance political agendas, cyberextortionists attack for personal gain. Extortion is when a criminal threatens an individual or a group with any form of attack. Before computers, this commonly took the form of physical violence or blackmail. Blackmail is when a criminal forces someone to do something by threatening to share sensitive information about the victim. In the online world, cyberextortion is the act of forcing someone to do something by using a computer. A cyberextortionist uses a form of malware called ransomware which, by the FBI's definition, "encrypts, or locks, valuable digital files and demands a ransom to release them."[8] A ransom is a payment made to an extortionist to unlock the files. Ransomware was well known in the early 2000s because of botnets that installed ransomware in sensitive networks, such as those of hospitals. In the 2010s, it has become a globally serious threat for its ability to attack wherever data storage is inadequately protected.

The largest, most ambitious ransomware attack in history occurred in 2017. After a group of anonymous hackers calling themselves the Shadow Brokers released a set of hacking tools supposedly stolen from the NSA, cybercriminals across the world began adapting the digital weapon immediately. Beginning in early May, tens of thousands of computers—including those used by hospitals in England and Russian government systems—were infected with a software that encrypted the machine's files and demanded a $300 payment to unlock them. The virus was spread through an e-mail attachment, and it spread to 150 countries within days. Just as quickly as the

Ransomware attacks on hospitals, such as in 2017, are frightening; if health care professionals cannot access their files, lives could be lost.

Sextortion

At the same time cyberextortion became a major threat to financial institutions, an equally harmful version—named sextortion—was used by cybercriminals to manipulate individuals into dangerous arrangements with them. In sextortion, the cyberextortionist befriends or deceives their victim under false pretenses. They often pose as someone else, such as a high school student, to obtain nude or revealing photographs of a person. They accomplish this by emotionally manipulating their victim.

Once they have these photos, they use them as leverage against their victim with the threat they will release them to friends, acquaintances, or on the Internet—unless the victim meets their demands. While adults of any gender are at risk, minors and females are statistically more targeted in sextortion cases. Across 800 tips received between 2013 and 2015, the National Center for Missing and Exploited Children found 78 percent of the sextortion victims were female.

When adults are the targets of sextortion, the criminal often wants money in exchange for their privacy. When children are targeted, however, "the offender in three-fourths of the cases was seeking more [inappropriate] material, rather than money."[1] In addition to being forced to continue taking compromising pictures or paying a ransom, victims of sextortion suffer extreme emotional and psychological trauma, which can lead some to self-harming. In 2015, an FBI investigation revealed that more than 28 percent of the cases they studied ended with a minor's suicide or attempted suicide. Government officials around the world have urged young Internet users to protect their privacy.

1. Tom Jackman, "'Sextortion,' growing online problem worldwide, victimizes two George Mason students," *The Washington Post*, May 10, 2016. www.washingtonpost.com/news/true-crime/wp/2016/05/10/sextortion-growing-online-problem-worldwide-victimizes-two-george-mason-students/?utm_term=.f85d30f9b214#comments.

attack spread, however, it came to an end. One researcher found a hidden switch in the virus's code that could shut it down—permanently. This could not cleanse the estimated 200,000 computers that had already been infected, but the virus was no longer able to spread. Though nations across the globe feared the consequences of the malware, the virus was contained and computers were protected.

By the Numbers

$450 billion

amount of money lost to cybercrime in 2016

What Statistics Do Not Show

Like with many forms of crime, statistics and definite numbers are often hard to determine when victims sometimes prefer to stay silent and not speak out. The full extent of cybercrime of any type can only be estimated, mainly due to the fact that many victims do not report such crimes. This is particularly true of potentially hazardous spam, in which computer users are overwhelmed with unwanted e-mails that try to get them to purchase a fake product, or visit a website that will cause a virus to download to their hard drive. The modern user receives so many spam e-mails that most just delete them without flagging them. Some who find themselves on a dangerous website, either by accident or on purpose, also are unlikely to report it in any way. Sextortion cases are often unreported as well, mostly because victims, who are frequently minors, are ashamed or embarrassed for sharing explicit pictures online. Some victims may even fear that they will get in trouble for their actions. In one effort to combat this trend, the FBI released a statement explaining that the government

> *does not treat a child as an offender in the production of [inappropriate pictures] as a result of their sextortion or coercion. In order for the victimization to stop, children typically have to come forward to someone—normally a parent, teacher, caregiver, or law enforcement. The embarrassment of the activity a child was forced to engage in is what typically prevents them from coming forward. Sextortion offenders may have hundreds of victims around the world, so coming forward to help law enforcement identify the offender may prevent countless other incidents of sexual exploitation to that victim and others.*[9]

Gathering accurate data on most types of cybercrime is also a challenge because, as Wall wrote, "information about reported victimization does not flow through a single portal such as the police in the same way as does reporting of street and related crime."[10] Wall also explained that there have been a number of academic studies on the phenomenon of cybercrime, but even the best of these studies are still just estimations of the true extent of cybercrime worldwide. What is obvious, however, is how costly cybercrime is to businesses.

"From 2013 to 2015 the cyber crime costs quadrupled, and it looks like there will be another quadrupling from 2015 to 2019,"[11] wrote one cybersecurity expert, in 2016. This would bring total costs to more than $2 trillion—a staggeringly high amount. He also reiterated that not all cybercrime can

By the Numbers

$3,718

average amount lost per cybercrime complaint in 2015

easily be discovered. Some companies may have had their data breached and not even realize it for months. "Large banks, retailers, and federal agencies make the headlines when they are hacked—but all businesses are at risk. According to Microsoft, 20% of small to mid sized businesses have been cyber crime targets."[12]

Digital Experts, Computer Forensics

Computer forensic specialists share many approaches with traditional crime scene investigators with one obvious exception: They mostly use electronic technology to do their jobs. In fact, many computer forensic detectives began their careers as traditional detectives. These forensic specialists are commonly part of a cybercrime unit that includes other team members from a law enforcement agency. Working together, they follow crime-solving procedures, much like any other type of investigators. Their mission is to identify and apprehend the suspect, gather and analyze the evidence and data, and build a case to put the perpetrator behind bars.

Chapter Two

The Internet as a Crime Scene

Though the techniques have become more digital, the general principles of crime solving are still relevant to cybercrime, and the first step is to identify those responsible. This would be nearly impossible for the investigators without the crimes being reported by victims, since only a small percentage of cybercrimes are discovered by authorities and operators before the victims. Some victims of cybercrime may not even know where to file a complaint, but the typical method is for private citizens to go to their local police. More knowledgeable Internet users alert the Internet Crime Complaint Center (IC3), while corporations might approach a federal agency, such as the FBI, the Internal Revenue Service (IRS), or the Federal Communications Commission (FCC).

Because the Internet flows through cyberspace across the world, there are many law enforcement organizations that attempt to control crime on both the national and international level. In the United States, cybercrime is a concern addressed by the following agencies: The FBI, which uses vast resources and thousands of experts in the field to coordinate information and planning among local and national agencies; the U.S. Department of Justice, which includes several divisions, including a team of some of the world's best computer scientists, that specifically target various cybercrimes, such as fraud, terrorism, violent crime, theft, and crimes against minors; the U.S. Department of Defense, which is primarily concerned with international terrorism and matters of national security, including those involving cybercrime; the National Security Agency (NSA), which is primarily concerned with threats involving terrorism, also gets involved in border control and other national issues, such as preventing and investigating cyberspace attacks; the IRS, which has a team in its Seized Computer Evidence Recovery

The FBI is in charge of many high-profile cybercrime cases. It employs some of the world's best cybersecurity experts.

unit; and the U.S. Drug Enforcement Administration (DEA), which uses a computer forensics unit to fight against organized drug dealing groups.

There are also a number of nongovernmental regulatory organizations that monitor the Internet, including the Internet Watch Foundation (IWF), the Coalition Against Unsolicited Commercial Email (CAUCE), and the Computer Emergency Response Team (CERT). The IWF is based in England

Though some American citizens have objected, the NSA has undertaken a large portion of the U.S. cyberdefense responsibility in recent years.

and it represents a cooperative effort between ISPs, police, and the government. CAUCE, which has branches in North America, Europe, Asia, and elsewhere, is a nonprofit group that focuses on preventing the spread of spam through the Internet. CERT, based at the Carnegie Mellon Software Engineering Institute in Pittsburgh, Pennsylvania, is a collaborative effort between the U.S. government and businesses to fight against viruses and other Internet malware.

All of these governmental and nonprofit organizations require the services of computer forensics specialists. As the rate and expense of cybercrime has skyrocketed in the 2010s, there are also a growing number of private companies that provide these services as well.

By the Numbers

$85.1 million

the FBI's 2017 budget request to improve its cyber investigation potential

Finding Holes

One of the understated roles of federal cybercrime divisions in the United States and other countries is to investigate the faults in major national computer networks to find where they are most vulnerable. Oftentimes, the holes are found before any major investigation, which leads to security concerns before attacks even occur. Michael V. Hayden, the former director of the NSA and Central Intelligence Agency (CIA), described one of the NSA's own network faults in his book *Playing to the Edge: American Intelligence in the Age of Terror*. Hayden told about the night the NSA's network crashed in 2000 as a result of a data storm, which is when data collections overwhelm a network that is not powerful enough to handle them.

> *Signals intelligence, or SIGNT, is a continuous process, a kind of espionage production line where communications are collected, processed, analyzed, and reported twenty-four hours a day. At that moment satellites and earthbound collection points around the world were still intercepting communications, their vast take—telephone calls, faxes, radio signals—still pouring into memory buffers. But once in hand, the data froze. We couldn't move it. Nobody could access it. Nobody could analyze it. It wouldn't take long for intelligence consumers to notice something was wrong. They could tell it when their morning take showed up light or didn't show up at all. For all intents and purposes, NSA was brain-dead.*[1]

This instance was neither the first nor the last network failure of any major American system, and while the systems were eventually repaired, the story could easily have resulted in a catastrophe. If a cyberattack was perpetrated at that period of vulnerability, the results could have been disastrous for America.

1. Michael V. Hayden, *Playing to the Edge: American Intelligence in the Age of Terror*. New York, NY: Penguin, 2016, p. 2.

Relying on Specialists

Cooperation between professionals with years of individual experience is how complex crimes are solved. However, though law enforcement agencies are becoming more and more experienced with computer forensics, there are times when not enough trained staff is available to tackle complex technical issues. Departments have grown and received greater funding in recent years, but many law enforcement agencies are underfunded. In areas where technological experts are not employed by the agencies, detectives and other investigators will turn to outside experts for help. The supervisor in charge of an investigation also must determine, however, if their department has the funds to pay an outside expert and whether coordinating with an outside forensic specialist is possible, given the sensitive nature of most cybercrime.

In addition to higher government sources, such as the FBI's Computer Analysis Response Team, investigators can also consult private corporations, such as Microsoft, Micro Focus, and Cisco. These companies hire some of the best computer experts in the world. They are familiar with specialized areas of computer science, and thus provide a valuable resource to investigators. There are even private firms that specialize in selling their computer security consultations. In either case, though, funding can be an issue if the law enforcement agency does not have a lot of money to spend. Because computer security is complex and in-demand, consultations can be highly expensive.

Despite the high price tag, however, "most private experts are not familiar with the judicial system [so] it is unlikely that the expert will know how to execute a search warrant ... or resolve search issues that may affect the evidence's [use in] trial. Thus, a private expert should be paired with an experienced agent every step of the way."[13]

Though no police agency would ever ask private citizens to get involved in crime-solving directly, some technologically advanced people help the government. Private individuals with computer expertise who gather evidence against cybercriminals and report it to the authorities are sometimes called cybersleuths. They are white hats who often believe the Internet belongs to the public and that it should be safe for all to navigate. A *New York Times* reporter captured the perspective of one cybersleuth: "'We felt the Internet belonged to us,' said [the] founder of ... a group that works with law enforcement to track down online [criminals]. 'Just like saying, "You're not going to sell crack on our corner," we don't want you to [commit crimes] on our Internet.'"[14]

In the history of computer security, there have undoubtedly been cases where cybersleuths have been a major help to government investigators. Despite their help—which is almost always given without cost—police do not like citizens getting involved in serious criminal matters. They worry about possible retaliation, corrupted data, or other safety concerns. For those reasons, as more private security firms and professional experts have spread in the 21st century, agencies have increasingly turned to them.

One of the most famous cases of a hacker being utilized by authorities is the life of James Kosta, who had hacked

Young computer enthusiasts can sometimes commit cybercrimes without even realizing what they are doing is wrong; often, these mistakes are harmless.

General Electric, IBM, and other major banks and networks by the time he was 14 years old. Kosta, who was initially sentenced to 45 years in prison on 45 counts of technical burglary, became an intelligence expert for the Navy at 18 and joined the CIA at 20. Kosta now runs multiple software and gaming companies, such as 3G Studios, and he encourages youth in positions similar to his to embrace their potential. His is the ultimate success story for young hackers: turning from a life of crime to a successful life on the right side of the law.

Breadcrumbs in Cyberspace

In the same way the Internet's general anonymity attracts new cybercriminals, lawmakers depend on the fact that criminals fear safeguards put in place by

Issues of Jurisdiction

Because a huge portion of cybercriminals attack beyond state and international borders, jurisdiction is a major issue when it comes to how computer crimes are prosecuted and which agencies have the power to investigate. The problem has made cooperation between various law enforcement agents all the more important, and has increased the intervention of federal agencies into crimes that normally would have been under local jurisdiction.

Despite the importance of working together, a lack of law-enforcement cooperation between jurisdictions is an ongoing problem that hampers multi-state investigations. The problem is compounded by local politics, budgets, resources, transparency, and rivalries between agencies. When foreign agencies become involved in an international investigation, the issue of cooperation is made all the more complicated. While computer crime investigators must always keep legal concerns about jurisdiction in mind when they are working on any case, agencies need to improve their teamwork so they can prevent more cybercrime.

security teams to keep a large portion of people from embracing cybercrime. This is one of the ways legislators and cybersecurity professionals try to keep up with criminals—relying on a fear of consequences while also adapting to new technology and new thinking.

Cybercriminals are well aware of the risks they take in perpetrating online fraud, carrying out computer attacks, or running websites with illegal content. They know that data about their activities is saved by ISPs and other companies that do business online. The government and law enforcement are aware of this, too, which is why laws have been put in place that require certain information to be stored for a certain amount of time and with certain levels of accessibility. This way, there is an existing record in case an investigation is needed. Even with this reasonable regulation, such records can be difficult for certain agencies to access due to restrictions, mishandling, and noncompliance.

Data retention is one of the most central parts of recent legislation regarding the protection and privacy of the Internet. Depending on the type of company hosting or dealing with information online, different laws apply. For example, publicly traded companies must adhere to the Sarbanes-Oxley Act when storing Internet data records, and health-care providers must adhere to the Health Insurance Portability and Accountability Act regarding electronic health-care data. Such laws make it

The Sarbanes-Oxley Act of 2002 marked a major turning point for both corporate responsibility and cybersecurity.

possible for law enforcement to use official orders to extract valuable electronic records for investigations.

There is, however, debate about maintaining sensitive financial information, such as credit card transactions, in company databases. There have been several cases of hackers cracking retailer, bank, and credit card company records to steal credit card numbers or customers' personal information. In 2013, Target stores suffered one of the largest and most widely publicized data breaches in history when hackers stole information about 40 million customers. This included names, addresses, birth dates, and credit card numbers. This had serious consequences for Target, their customers, and other retailers across the globe. If a large company could be attacked effectively, what stops hackers from taking even more data again?

Occupation: Network Security Systems Manager

Job Description:
A network security systems manager is responsible for keeping computer networks at a company or other organization safe from external or internal attacks that may damage or destroy valuable data or put that data at risk. This position typically oversees the operations of local area networks (LAN), wide area networks (WAN), and other informational systems, such as telephone networks. A network security manager typically has a staff of information technology professionals and is responsible for planning and implementing security strategies.

Education:
At minimum, network security managers require a bachelor's degree in computer science, information technology, or a field related to online security. Many companies prefer a master's degree, with an extra focus on cybersecurity.

Qualifications:
Experience in the information technology field, preferably in the area of large-scale security, is required. Potential network security systems managers must have computer programming skills and staff management credentials and be familiar with the latest in cutting-edge security technology advances.

Salary:
In 2017, the average salary of a network security systems manager was $97,850.

Concerns about customer confidentiality have caused states to pass and continue to refine laws which force companies to delete credit card information after a transaction has been completed, or to take other steps, such as ensuring that electronic transactions are securely encrypted. This way, no information is available for hackers to find. Businesses have been resistant to such legislation because it costs them a great deal more money and work to ensure the confidentiality of their customers' information. For example, in California, where the computer industry is centered, businesses and companies often avoided the costs of certain safeguards, such as deleting customer information. They were able to do this until 2014, when California governor Jerry Brown signed AB 1710, which requires certain companies to maintain reasonable security procedures and practices in storing personal information. Businesses must also disclose information about data breaches and provide free identity theft mitigation for 12 months. Even after the law went into effect, major corporations have resisted its implementation. Though upgrading security measures would cost these companies a lot of money, it would also help protect the identity and personal information of their customers.

Methods for Masking

From the most basic anti-abuse programs on social media networks to the advanced spyware at the disposal of most government cybersecurity programs, computers and the Internet no longer promise absolute anonymity to general users—let alone cybercriminals. Someone hoping to commit a digital crime must go through a number of complicated strategies to hide their identities and their activities. In the case of online money laundering, often part of credit card identity theft and fraud, they may hide information in databases maintained in other countries. Remote databases hide not only information, but also online hosting companies from other nations. This is a frequent strategy of hackers, who set up botnets in one country by attacking victims' computers from foreign locations.

Another method is to convert money into difficult-to-trace digital currency. Digital currencies, such as Bitcoin, Ethereum, and Litecoin, allow people to buy online currency anonymously, which can then be traded and used similarly to real cash. While some consumers believe that this gives them a higher level of security and anonymity, digital currency can be dangerous. It is prone is losing value quickly, similar to the stock market, and skilled hackers could break into databases and leave people penniless. Additionally, cybercriminals can convert their stolen money into digital currency, which makes them nearly untraceable.

Computers connected to the Internet use Transmission Control Protocol (TCP) and Internet Protocol (IP) to communicate with each other and with network servers. This standardized protocol makes it possible for the computer to communicate with any hosting network server. Each computer user has a unique IP address, which is registered and includes a user's address, phone number, and name. Hackers and other knowledgeable cybercriminals know this, and they employ strategies to hide this information. They use IP addresses that cannot be traced back to them, which allow them to remain anonymous. One way of hiding online activity is to connect via a virtual private network (VPN). These

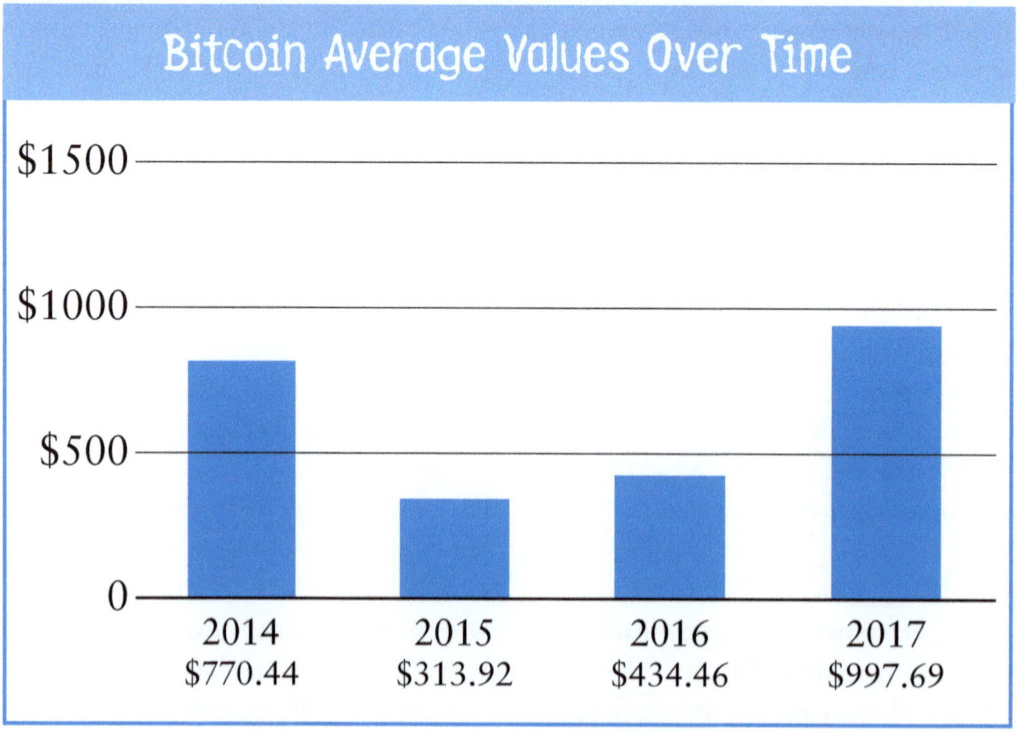

Though Bitcoins are the most popular form of digital currency because they allow confidentiality, their value is highly vulnerable to sharp changes.

networks route a user's connection to an encrypted, secured location, which is maintained by the VPN provider. This makes it so their browsing history and other personal information is not easily accessible.

Cybercriminals can also route their Internet traffic through a proxy server, which acts as an intermediary between two servers. When this is done, the IP address that is stored on the destination server is that of the proxy server, not the original IP address belonging to the criminal. This is a particularly common strategy for criminals using Internet relay chat, since these chat tools are difficult to track and are a known avenue for cybercriminals to distribute malware across the Internet.

Tracking the Anonymous

NCovert, which has been around since the early 2000s, is a program designed to hide criminals' identities. It works by using "spoofing techniques to hide the source of communications and the data that travels over the network."[15] Spoofing is a term referring to the methods used by hackers or other cybercriminal to hide their true identity in an e-mail or website. NCovert allows potential cybercriminals to almost disappear from the Internet whenever they are using it. Privacy advocates have argued that such programs allow people to protect themselves online. Others, however, have argued that it gives cybercriminals too much power while simultaneously lowering their risk of capture.

While not all programs similar to NCovert were designed purely for criminal purposes, they have certainly been used for them. One prominent example is Tor, which was actually developed by the U.S. government. Tor is an acronym for "the Onion Router," a downloadable software which allows users to cover their tracks by passing information through several relay points, referred to as nodes, to conceal their identity. Nodes do the same work one proxy server does, but many times over, removing layers of encryption as data passes through each node until eventually data is delivered between servers without being tracked. Tor operates via its own nearly untraceable browser, where users can create webpages that are hidden from standard searches and typical government surveillance methods. These websites are often used to hide infamous black markets that would be inaccessible without the Tor browser.

Although some see Tor as a tool to liberate Internet users in the face of what they believed were unethical violations of browsing privacy, the fact remains it is often used for illegal activities. One key example is when Timothy DeFoggi, former director of cybersecurity at the U.S. Department of Health and Human Services, was arrested and sentenced to 25 years on child pornography charges in 2015. DeFoggi used Tor and his expertise as a cybersecurity professional to hide his activity for years, and the only way the FBI was able to catch him was by using Tor themselves to stealthily track and investigate DeFoggi. "Agents added Flash software to [a] site ... If visitors used an outdated version of Tor—and didn't set their computers to block Flash—that Flash app was able to establish a direct connection and reveal their IP address,"[16] journalist Jose Pagliery explained.

IP addresses cause some of the biggest challenges to law enforcement officials. There are two kinds of IP addresses: static and dynamic. Static IP addresses are the norm for people using e-mail and Internet browsers in a fixed location, such as a home or business. Because people are becoming increasingly mobile—accessing the Internet through laptops, smartphones, and other electronic communication devices—ISPs are more routinely assigning users IPs that change each time they log into a different network system. Cybercriminals and cyberterrorists are often able to work quickly

Tor is the most famous browser for anonymous Internet use, but it has drawn criticism because of its potential applications for cybercriminals.

by utilizing public computers and not concealing their IP address, since the government would track the IP address back to the public computer—but by the time they do that, the criminal has fled and there is nothing to connect them to the crime.

Another challenge for investigators tracking e-mails, specifically, is that e-mails are routed through the Internet through different paths, depending on Internet traffic. All digital communications, including e-mails, are assigned media access control (MAC) addresses

How Investigators Track Computers

An IP address (which is expressed digitally as a string of numbers, such as 15.342.7.455) is an extremely valuable tool for cybercrime investigators. This address, which is unique to every computer, includes identifying data, such as the town where the computer is located, the ISP for that computer, and the exact coordinates of the house or business registered to that number.

ISPs maintain a database that records each registered IP address and who registered the address. When someone visits a website, the website automatically places a tag on the user. Detectives can obtain IP addresses through these unique tags and then access information that could prove criminal activity. Skilled criminals, however, can hide their IP addresses to trick investigators and disguise their identities.

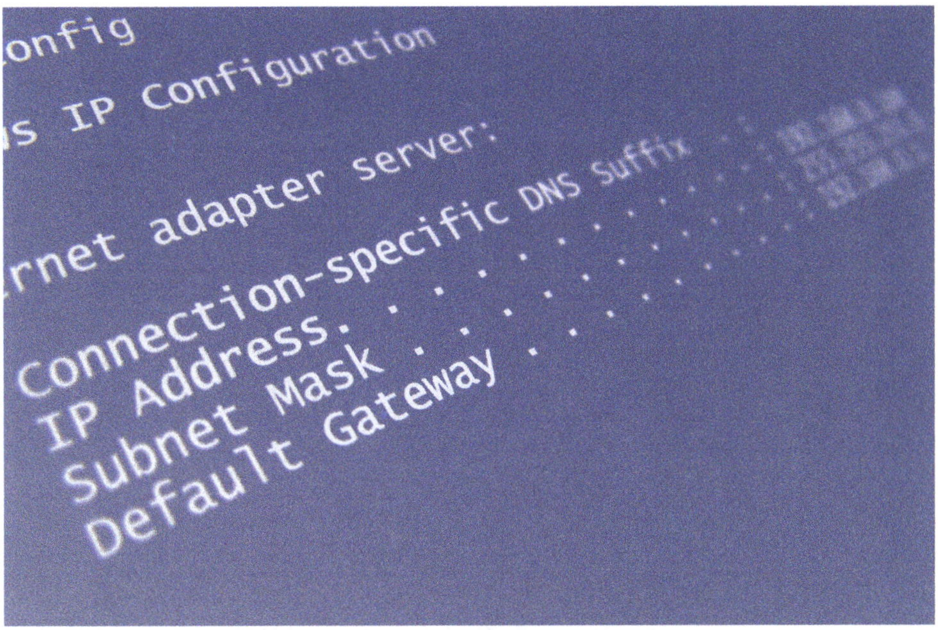

IP addresses can lead investigators directly to a hacker—or send them on a chase around the world with no results.

as they travel through cyberspace. These MAC addresses contain important information that tell the communication where to go. For example, if computer A wanted to send an e-mail to computer B, the information in the MAC address would include the MAC addresses of both A and B. However, as one expert explained,

> *network communications rarely take place directly from one end point to another. They typically bounce off a series of routers on the way to their destination. In order for this to happen, the [information] needs to be updated at each router with the MAC address of the next router ... by the time the [information] reaches its destination, the MAC addresses ... have changed several times, making it a bad indicator of origin.*[17]

As a result, the message from A will have countless other bits of information before it reaches B, which means that investigators will find it incredibly difficult—if not impossible—to use the MAC address to trace computer A and whoever may have been using it.

Monitoring Websites

While ISPs and other companies that provide online services are not able to see every piece of information that goes across their networks, they are valuable tools for monitoring online activity. One example is the online auction website eBay. Each user's IP is registered at an ISP. This data is, in turn, maintained by the American Registry for Internet Numbers (ARIN), which hosts these numbers online. A court order is necessary to obtain records from an ISP. Matching information from other sources, such as ARIN, with data from an ISP can be an effective tool in cornering a suspect or narrowing down an investigation.

Fraud committed via websites similar to eBay is an ongoing problem on the Internet, and even though online marketplaces monitor their website to the best of their abilities, there are still disreputable dealers who do not deliver promised goods to auction winners. Unfortunately for law enforcement, tracking down these fraudsters is an extremely difficult and complicated process. In one early example from 2000, eBay and IC3 received several tips about one particular online seller:

> *To hide his identity, the seller used a Hotmail account for online communications and several mail drops to receive checks. Logs obtained from Hotmail revealed that the seller was accessing the Internet through a subsidiary of Uunet. When served with a [court order], Uunet disclosed the suspect's MSN account and associated address, credit card and telephone numbers.*[18]

Even with this information, investigators still had to cross-reference what they learned with data from eBay, the suspect's bank, employees who worked at the suspect's mail drop locations, and real estate records.

Law enforcement agencies work to improve their cybersecurity software every single day so they can better fight cybercriminals.

After comparing all this information in a labor-intensive investigation, police were finally led to the suspect's secret alternate address, where they were able to locate the scammer. In the years since this particular case, making oneself anonymous on the Internet has become infinitely more complex, meaning that investigators are forced to do increasingly more work with each case.

Other electronic sources are available to investigators that may even be more useful than ISP data, particularly network systems managed by private corporations. In the 21st century, as nearly every aspect of life becomes digitized, corporate networks commonly maintain records in

> *databases, document management systems, time clock systems, and other networked systems that contain information about the individuals who use them. Also, private organizations often configure their networks to monitor individuals' activities more than the public Internet. Some organizations monitor which Web pages were accessed from computers on their networks. Other organizations even go so far as to analyze the raw traffic flowing through their network for signs of suspicious activity.*[19]

There is also the Internet Assigned Numbers Authority, which is a resource computer forensic specialists use to find domain name system (DNS) information to track cybercriminals. The DNS is a database maintained by the Internet Corporation for Assigned Names and Numbers. It includes information on who registered which website, and it details both the domain name URL (Uniform Resource Locator) address (for example, www.sampleaddress.com) and the numeric address identifier, which is the address computers use to communicate the location of a website to each other. Investigators can use either the URL or the numeric identifier to discover the owner of the website they are seeking information about.

Discovering the address of an ISP can help trace a criminal to their geographical location. According to experts,

> *addresses are important [because] they will show the methods used by the computer suspect to commit the acts in question. For instance, in mail scams … the DNS, URL, or IP addresses are normally faked or run through various cover addresses. It usually takes awhile, but even with simple programs … the investigator can find a surprising number of links back to the suspect.*

Knowing those addresses, how they are created, and how they are used in the larger system is a key to being able to track the suspect.[20]

By the Numbers

$16 billion

amount of money lost due to identity fraud of U.S. consumers in 2016

E-mails Provide a Record

Despite efforts to conceal their movements, even the most skilled cybercriminals leave a trail of evidence as they send e-mails through the Internet. Talented forensic investigators will follow this trail, in addition to website tracking, as a major investigative tool.

Cybercriminals try to hide their identities when they send spam or e-mails with malware attachments, primarily by using special commands to access other computers remotely using the Internet's Simple Mail Transfer Protocol (SMTP). The SMTP does not require user identification, so hackers can send e-mails without authentic identifiers. Most e-mail users never see the identifier code attached to their e-mails, but disguising or altering this code allows hackers to fake the "from" field so that an e-mail appears to originate from someone legitimate, rather than a criminal.

E-mail headers contain important information, such as the exact date and time an e-mail was sent to the recipient, the return path (the e-mail address to which an e-mail is sent if the recipient replies), the address of the server hosting the e-mail program, and the addresses of any other e-mail servers through which the e-mail traveled. Most of this information can be altered by a skilled cybercriminal. What a hacker cannot easily hide, however, is the IP address identifying the originator. Though it still takes a lot of investigating to uncover this crucial IP address, it can give a computer forensic specialist a solid lead.

To discover IP information, investigators may examine the SMTP server log that is maintained by the mail server's hosting company. Server logs maintain data about e-mails as well, including originating IPs and message dates. According to one expert, "the server log is actually a better source of details than the message [itself], and the investigator [should] gain cooperation from the ISP or other server host."[21]

Trying to identify a cybercriminal

by tracing their activities on the Internet is comparable to narrowing down suspects in a traditional crime: It is just the first step in the long process of solving the case. Where cybercrime differentiates itself, however, is that cyberspace investigators rarely have much evidence on which to base their investigations compared to crimes that happen in the real world. Creating a list of cybercrime suspects is challenging enough—and the investigation only gets tougher from there.

By the Numbers

15.4 million

number of American identity fraud victims in 2016

Chapter Three
Tracking the Suspects

The process of solving a cybercrime is long, complex, and requires dozens of workers. Identifying potential suspects is just the first step in a long journey for law enforcement officials. The next step is where the case can be made—or destroyed. After investigators have a strong reason to suspect someone in particular, they must gather evidence, both digital and physical, and analyze it. Before pursuing anyone past this stage, police need to be confident about who the cybercriminal is; if they chase the wrong person, they could waste hundreds of hours and a lot of money. If their evidence and analysis point toward the right person, law enforcement then take steps to trap the criminal. There are countless ways to capture a cybercriminal in virtual space, including: sniffers, keyloggers, cookies, and honeypots.

Surveillance Software

While intelligence agencies and law enforcement are most often forced to use the same technology as cybercriminals, sometimes going undercover to do so, there are various legitimate software programs available to them for surveillance. Just as with traditional surveillance methods, such as video or voice recorders, investigators typically need a warrant before monitoring a suspect's computer. Exceptions to this rule might be cases involving national security, which are too important to not act on immediately.

There are a number of computer programs, used both by law enforcement and private citizens, that can be used for snooping on other people's computer activity. Programs called sniffers are employed for both legal and illegal purposes. A sniffer program can monitor any kind of traffic—including e-mail, file downloads, and more—entering or leaving a computer that is attached to a network. Companies might use sniffer programs to monitor employee behavior; cybercriminals can use them to record and steal personal data; and law enforcement agencies use sniffers to discover criminal behavior.

Because of the way computers work when attached to a network, a sniffer can detect the information transmitted between them:

> *A network sniffer monitors data flowing over computer network links in real time ... Also sometimes called "network probes" or "snoops," sniffers monitor network traffic, tanking snapshot copies of the data but without redirecting it or altering it ... Sniffers can only intercept data from the networks their host computer is attached to.*[22]

Sniffers tell network servers that the standard practice of ignoring data traffic from other computers should be reversed. Then, someone connected to the network can use a sniffer, which will allow them to see everything traveling through the network. Sniffers also can detect the type of protocol being used (such as e-mail or Internet browsing protocols); therefore, the program can read the content and the information about the source of the data that was generated. This makes sniffers a powerful tool for investigating potential cybercrimes.

There are a number of different programs that function as sniffers for investigators and security experts. Some are optimized to work on certain operating

Apple and Microsoft make the most popular operating systems in the world, and their architectures are very different. Programs must be specially created to work with either.

systems, such as Windows or Macintosh, while others are for general use. Modern sniffer tools can be so powerful that they actually give investigators too much data; there are other tools, called sifters, that help them sort through the results to find relevant information.

Network administrators frequently use sniffer programs legitimately to gather data about Internet usage at, for example, a business office. There is another side of sniffer tools, however—if investigators can use sniffers to discover Internet activity, so can cybercriminals. There are dozens of easily obtainable sniffer programs online, and an experienced hacker is capable of writing their own. Moreover, while an investigator has a hard time searching through vast data returns from their sniffer tools, a hacker can target their search to discover personal information, such as login credentials for bank websites, without getting overloaded with data.

By the Numbers

4.2 billion

number of records exposed due to data breaches in 2016

Tracking Typing

Many computer users are aware of software designed to monitor keystrokes. Keylogging software, as it is called, is a much more direct means of gathering data from a computer: It monitors and records what a person is typing on the keyboard. There are hundreds of different programs that function as keyloggers, and many are not made to be used for crime. Some allow users, often parents, to observe the computer activity of their children. These programs have stealth settings so the person whose activities are being recorded is not aware of the program being active on their computer. The keylogging software then creates a report, which is secretly e-mailed to a specific address. Outside of parental use, both cybercriminals and law enforcement officers make use of keylogging programs.

The most common way criminals abuse keyloggers is by installing them onto personal computers without the knowledge of the user. This is often accomplished by e-mailing or uploading a virus. When the criminal receives the report from the software, they can typically trace their victim's login information for any number of websites—including banks, online retailers, and the government. They can then use this information to steal money, credit card numbers, and even someone's identity.

To fight against this, law enforcement

agencies can also use keyloggers to track cybercrime. As hackers use increasingly sophisticated encryption methods to conceal the data they are gathering or transmitting, a keylogger can be a useful tool to obtain the information investigators need directly. If security teams can trace the keystrokes of a hacker, they can figure out how they are programming their next attack and then develop defenses against it. A clumsy hacker could even reveal their personal identity without even knowing it.

The first known case of law enforcement using a keylogging program was in 1999, when Nicodemo Scarfo Jr., a mob boss in New Jersey, was arrested on charges for murder, attempted murder,

Nicodemo Scarfo Jr. was the first American criminal to be arrested due to evidence that was collected by government software.

How Cookies Work

Cookies, also called Internet cookies or browser cookies, are packets of text information that contain information about a computer user's machine. When a user visits a website on the Internet, the website transmits a cookie, which is stored in the user's computer. Each time the visitor returns to that website, the cookie identifies them as someone who has been to the website before. This is useful for features such as online forms and shopping carts, where data, such as names and addresses, can be automatically filled in because the information is already stored.

Cookies are standard parts of Internet use in the 21st century, and they do not spread viruses or other malware, as some people falsely believe. However, there can still be some risks, especially if a person is on a public or shared computer. If a user enters personal data at a website, then others who share that computer could potentially visit the same website and learn the first user's personal information. Moreover, privacy advocates argue that some companies may collect data from their digital visitors and then sell this data to others, thus encouraging spam e-mail.

and other serious crimes. The FBI obtained a court order to enter Scarfo's home and install a keylogger, as well as other detection software, onto his home computer. This allowed the FBI to uncover Scarfo's passwords and access data he had been hiding in his electronic files. At the time, the FBI was able to circumvent legal questions because President Bill Clinton's administration had worked to change federal laws, allowing more freedom for investigations and operations that included secretly entering and surveilling the homes of suspected criminals.

Since the terrorist attacks of September 11, 2001, federal laws have been revised and expanded even more to allow similar searches. In 2016, the Supreme Court of the United States gave lower-level judges extensive powers to order searches of suspected criminals' computers, even across state and national borders. While some have insisted that these changes will improve cybersecurity, others argue that they give the government far too much power to look into people's personal information.

Federal Tracking Tech

Complicated technologies have been developed by the government in the past to snag cybercriminals. Carnivore, for example, was one of the first programs developed by the FBI to monitor Internet activity. First developed during President Clinton's administration, Carnivore used Windows operating systems and had to be physically installed onto a network computer. Once the Carnivore user was granted administrator rights to the network, they had one of the most useful, and controversial, digital investigation tools of the U.S. government. "For instance, he or she can access the content of all communications, and change and edit files at will. What is more, anyone logged in as administrator can hide any evidence of the activity,"[23] according to one computer security expert. It would be possible for someone who hacked into a system using Carnivore to tamper with evidence, plant false leads, or extract confidential information for bribery, extortion, fraud, and more.

Carnivore was a government secret until 2000, when Congress called for an investigation into its use. The

The NSA is involved in nearly all aspects of the cybersecurity of the United States and its citizens, and the agency has both supporters and critics.

program brought up the serious question of ethics, privacy, and legality, since the methods used to obtain data using Carnivore might not have been admissible in a court of law. Carnivore's own security was called into question, as well, when it was discovered that technical issues with the software put it in jeopardy of being hacked by outside users. Nevertheless, the power of this software program made it an irresistible tool for law enforcement until it was eventually replaced by NarusInsight in 2005. In the 2010s, the government has a number of tools it can use to monitor, protect, and investigate crimes, though many of these programs remain a secret.

Using a program called Echelon, federal officials in the United States, Canada, England, Australia, and New Zealand also take advantage of the international nature of the Internet and monitor e-mails, telephone conversations, faxes, and other communications transmitted through global satellites. Echelon is mostly supervised by the National Security Agency, and it has been the subject of criticism from other nations who claim it violates people's rights and can be used for corporate espionage, such as stealing trade secrets. Despite occasional resistance, the Echelon program still operates to protect the security of hundreds of millions of citizens.

Software Crisis

Some of the other issues of debate when investigators and other authorities seek help from outside experts are the ethics of federal authority and how much power it should have. In 2015, after Syed Rizwan Farook and Tashfeen Malik (known as the San Bernardino killers) massacred 14 people in California, the FBI sought help from Apple to decrypt Farook's cell phone in an effort to find out more about potential connections to radical terrorist groups and bring any additional suspects in for investigation. Upon being requested to help decrypt the phone or to construct software for the FBI to do it, Apple's representatives, along with experts from Facebook and other Silicon Valley companies, were reluctant to help due to issues of privacy. They widely considered it unethical for the government to be able to spy on users.

A federal court ruling, made by U.S. Magistrate Sheri Pym, directed Apple to provide software to unlock the phone. The company refused and appealed to defend the privacy of its users as well as its own interests. The CEO of Apple, Tim Cook, wrote

> *Smartphones, led by iPhone, have become an essential part of our lives. People use them to store an incredible amount of personal information, from our private*

Some believe Apple CEO Tim Cook prioritized the rights of users in refusing the FBI, while others believed this obstructed an important investigation.

conversations to our photos, our music, our notes, our calendars and contacts, our financial information and health data …

All that information needs to be protected from hackers and criminals who want to access it, steal it, and use it without our knowledge or permission. Customers expect Apple and other technology companies to do everything in our power to protect their personal information, and at Apple we are deeply committed to safeguarding their data.[24]

The matter was closed on March 28, when the FBI got help from another software company to crack the passcode.

The U.S. government's reliance on certain companies and individuals is nothing new in the realm of cybercrime and cyberterrorism, but the debate over certain spyware is stronger than ever as a result. People have either heavily criticized or strongly supported Apple's decision to not unlock the phone. Supporters believe they were protecting the civil rights of billions of global users, while critics argue that the company slowed down an investigation that could have exposed further terrorist attacks.

Phishing for Cybercriminals

While some software remains undisclosed, government agencies, including the FBI and the NSA, can surveil the Internet and other computer networks in a passive form of data collection used for criminal investigations. Another method is to actually lure cybercriminals into traps similar, for example, to those criminals themselves use to lure their victims into online scams. In a practice called phishing, they can, for instance, create fake websites that attract people for one reason or another. One example is a website that mimics the appearance of a real bank's website. E-mails are sent out to the bank's customers, prompting them to click a link to the fraudulent bank website. They are then asked to input important data, such as credit card information or bank login credentials, which the cybercriminal then collects. Other examples include websites that ask people to input sensitive personal information. The best defense against phishing is to keep important information secret.

The same strategy is also used by law enforcement agencies. For instance, law enforcement technicians may create a website designed to attract people who are interested in purchasing illegal weapons. When someone enters the website, they are offered several chances to opt out of accessing the website's information. For example, the first page of the website could explain what the content is and then ask the website visitor if they wish to proceed by clicking an "accept" button. Several more pages may give the website visitor additional chances to leave the website before proceeding. If that person repeatedly provides personal information and clicks the "accept" buttons, they eventually come to a page that states the website is run by a law enforcement agency and that the visitor's activities have been monitored.

Equally as often, law enforcement officials are left with no choice but to operate undercover using the same software and manipulating the same digital rings as cybercriminals. In 2013, the FBI caught Ross William Ulbricht, the man accused of creating an illegal, multimillion-dollar e-commerce

Although government cybersurveillance has been criticized as invasive to privacy, it is an essential part of cyber investigations.

website named Silk Road. This website, hidden from most Internet users because it was invisible to search engines such as Google, allowed people to buy illegal drugs, sell illegal guns, and even pay to have someone killed—and do it completely anonymously. To catch Ulbricht and shut down the Silk Road server, the FBI's cybercrime specialists admitted to monitoring online forums and receiving records from Google, which traced Ulbricht through his VPN. While VPNs are typically extremely good at hiding IP addresses, the FBI used the forums posts and other data to cross-reference their information and track the VPN to a public computer, where they confirmed

Occupation: Security Software Developer

Job Description:
A developer (or coder) of security software uses a wide variety of software tools to create, test, and install new digital security systems. This position is found in law enforcement, the government, and private corporations. Security coders typically either work for a single employer or sell their services to the highest bidder on a case-by-case basis.

Education:
The minimum requirements to become a security software developer are a bachelor's degree in computer science, information technology, or a related field, with an emphasis on creating code and experience with developing software.

Qualifications:
Most employers looking for security software developers are interested in their ability to create new security procedures. This means coders must be skilled in a number of programming languages and be comfortable putting those skills to the test every day. Coding is a highly competitive field, and on-the-job experience or a master's degree can make candidates more desirable.

Salary:
In 2017, the average salary for a security software developer was $114,201.

Ulbricht had been logging into his e-mail account and using the VPN to monitor Silk Road's illegal activity.

A Sweet Net

A honeypot is any sophisticated system—a computer, an online space, or even a set of computer files and folders—that pretends to be a system that a hacker would want to break into. It is a deliberate setup intended for an outside hacker to crack into, which either records the hacker's break-in methods for later analysis by a computer forensic specialist or allows investigators to trace the source of the attack as it takes place. Such entrapment, when conducted by private individuals or companies, is widely considered to be against American federal regulations on surveillance. Creating a honeypot system is a time-consuming method that is primarily used for long-term investigations, such as attempting to catch a group of cybercriminals over a period of time. Investigators, upon discovering one criminal, are often forced to monitor their continued illegal activities to identify as many cybercriminals as possible to prevent accomplices from establishing countermeasures.

According to the Honeynet Project, a nonprofit research organization dedicated to making the Internet a safer place,

> *a Honeynet is a type of honeypot. Specifically, it is … designed to capture extensive information on threats … A Honeynet provides real systems, applications, and services for attackers to interact with … It is through this extensive interaction we gain information on threats, both external and internal to an organization. What makes a Honeynet different from most honeypots is that it is an entire network of systems … These victim systems (honeypots within the Honeynet) can be any type of system, service, or information you want to provide.*[25]

Because they are designed to be intentionally attacked, honeypots and honeynets can be risky when installed on other networks. To help protect the network, programs are installed that limit what a hacker can do to alter or extract network files and programs. By creating false systems to attract hackers and viruses, organizations such as the Honeynet Project can learn important information about how hackers work, and this data can then be shared with the government and private users to increase cybersecurity worldwide. However, in the 21st century, cybercriminals seem to be adapting more rapidly than ever before—and countermeasures are struggling to keep up.

The Transition to Wireless Surveillance

The explosive spread of wireless networks has created yet another challenge for law enforcement. Networks have almost entirely abandoned physical connections of cables and phone lines in favor of wireless connection. Wireless networks have the advantage of not being burdened by clumsy cords, but they can be particularly vulnerable to attack. They are easily accessed because hackers do not need a physical connection to enter a wireless network; they just need to be in range of the transmitting signal. Also, data transferred between computers on a wireless network is not perfectly encrypted. A 2007 survey conducted by the security company AirDefense studied more than 3,000 U.S. retail stores and found that 25 percent of them "were using an outdated encryption method [that] is easily cracked by thieves using widely

Many consumer wireless routers and modems, such as this one, are still only secured using WEP keys. This puts them at risk of cyberattack.

available tools."[26] Though security and hackers have each grown much more complex since 2007, many retailers and personal Internet users still have no idea how to set up their networks to properly protect their information. It is important to understand the difference between data encryption protocols on wireless networks for users to be safe from different forms of attack.

The original major public form of wireless network protection was named Wired Equivalent Privacy (WEP). Though relatively secure for a few years, it was soon replaced by Wi-Fi Protected Access (WPA), which had more sophisticated data encryption methods and was widely considered a significant upgrade in a number of aspects, including user authentication. Under WPA protection, each packet of data from each signal in a wireless network is encrypted with its own unique key, and each key is created and checked by four different algorithms. An algorithm is a set of rules in how something is calculated when solving problems. In the field of computers, algorithms are advanced formulas and codes, written into certain software by programmers and scientists to create an automatic function for that software.

WPA became widely used in in the early 2000s before it was replaced by WPA2 in 2004, which soon became the standard for wireless networks and is still seen in common use. WPA2 implements password protection in addition to the encryption algorithms run by its predecessor. Specifically, WPA2 on wireless networks that maintain mobile devices, home Wi-Fi routers and certain iCloud functions, uses improved algorithms to protect user data.

While certain cyber decryption methods—known as replay attacks—have been created to run advanced algorithms for password cracking and network intrusion, WPA2's encryption methods use greater processing power to fight this vulnerability. WPA2 is far from perfect, however, and one of its greatest weaknesses is "unauthorized access to the ... wireless network, where there is an invasion of ... certain Wi-Fi Protected Setup (WPS) access points. This can take the invader several hours of concerted effort with state-of-the-art computer technology, but the threat of system compromise should not be discounted."[27] One of the greatest challenges in cybersecurity is keeping a network safe, and thousands of professionals work to create new, protected methods of accessing the Internet.

Wi-Fi and Mobile Vulnerabilities

Following the massive rise of the Internet for more and more pieces of daily life, modern-day cybercrime and cyberterrorism take advantage of the fact that even major government systems can be vulnerable to attack. Since the beginning of the 2010s, the rising dependence on smartphones has, in turn, led to the creation of new viruses which attack the vulnerabilities of routers, passwords, photo libraries, cloud data storage and anything in the Internet of Things (IoT). IoT is a concept that refers to the present and future of device connectivity, in which nearly any electronic item can be interconnected in new ways through the Internet.

Mobile devices are less vulnerable to destructive ransomware because many advanced devices back their data up in other sources. So, if a virus encrypted the data on someone's phone, all that person would have to do is cleanse the software and re-download their information. (Though this is also possible with home computers, few users actively back up their data regularly like smartphones do automatically.) There are still some examples of phones or tablets being attacked by ransomware, but these attacks are generally less invasive when compared to other vulnerabilities in mobile

Vulnerabilities in smartphone technology are steadily rising. All users are encouraged to practice good security habits on every device.

technology. One example is the widely known Stagefright Android crisis that emerged in 2015.

The Stagefright bug, as it was named, bypassed security protocols by taking advantage of a small, almost invisible error in the Android operating system's coding. If a video with a virus were sent via text message, certain apps would immediately open the file without running a security check. This could potentially attack a user's phone before they could stop it, and more than 1 billion devices were at risk.

In response to this potential crisis, Android's operating system received several security improvements immediately and users have been receiving more frequent updates in the years since Stagefright. Nearly all mobile devices, including both Apple and

Ethics in Privacy

A number of federal laws have been passed over the years in an attempt to anticipate the potential abuses against personal privacy that electronic surveillance might impose. One of the most important laws is the Electronic Communications Privacy Act of 1986. The act is intended to cover all types of electronic communications, including wired and wireless forms, and provides guidance as to what is and is not allowed when it comes to intercepting, accessing, and reporting data transmitted between private individuals or corporations. The law specifically prohibits government agencies from seizing such data without following proper procedures.

During President Barack Obama's administration, a federal ISP regulation was proposed: Internet companies would need the explicit permission of their customers if they wanted to sell usage data to other corporations. The FCC approved this regulation in 2016, giving ISPs one year to comply with the new rules. When Donald Trump became president, however, this rule was repealed. On March 23, 2017, the U.S. Senate voted 50–48 to prevent these privacy measures from taking place. A large portion of America was outraged to hear this, because their private information—including browsing history, location, and Internet cookies—was now going to be sold without their consent.

Android products, have monthly or weekly updates where the user shuts down their phone for a few minutes while it reboots with more protection in addition to any other new features.

Undercover Digital Investigating

Not all digital investigating involves computer programming. In some situations, more traditional methods can be effective. An old and effective strategy that works particularly well in capturing potential online sex offenders and cyberbullies is for law enforcement to go undercover. This takes advantage of the fact that it is simple to assume a false identity while using the Internet, especially with the rise of social media websites such as Facebook and Twitter. A law enforcement agent poses, for example, as an underage teen or child and then allows a suspect to talk to them online. Thinking that the other person online is really a child, the potential cyberbully or molester will reveal information that is crucial to an investigation. The criminal might even set up a face-to-face meeting with the person they think is a child, and thus be easily captured by police.

By the Numbers

90

percentage of American adults who use Internet connections as of 2017

There are countless cases of law enforcement agents going undercover to prevent a cybercrime or catch a criminal. However, as hackers and technology have advanced and improved, it is increasingly more difficult for government agents to conceal their identity from an experienced professional cybercriminal. Just as the FBI and other investigative groups can trace an IP address to a criminal's location, a criminal could trace the undercover operative's IP address to find out they are really working for a government body. They can then easily destroy evidence or simply stop communicating. Online law enforcement is an immensely challenging task.

Chapter Four
Evidence Is Everything

Cyberinvestigators, particularly those involved with long-term investigations, are comfortable making an arrest if, and only if, they have collected enough evidence to ensure that a case can be made in a court of law against the cybercriminal. They need to make sure that they undoubtedly have the right person, and that a jury will see an overwhelming display of guilt. Otherwise, a cybercriminal might go free.

The amount of data available from tracing a lawbreaker through cyberspace is fairly limited, even after decades of advances in technology—but it is still a vital start to proving guilt. The original computer used by the perpetrator provides a lot of information. Some of this data, if not deleted by the computer user, is most easily found in the online browser history and temporary Internet files. Most cybercriminals, though, are experienced and intelligent enough to delete this information. Fortunately, incriminating files might still be saved in hidden places, such as the computer's hard drive or website connection logs, that are less easily removed. Even files that have been deleted leave fragments behind that can be pieced together by a talented investigator. For this reason, it is important for everyone—not just cybercriminals—to remember that anything posted online will be there forever. While this argument is sometimes simply a warning against sharing too much information on social media, the same logic is true of more serious crimes on the Internet.

Most of the basic procedures in obtaining evidence for a conviction still apply despite how cybercrime continues to evolve in the eyes of law enforcement. Investigators who have identified possible suspects in a computer crime will often desire two types of evidence: physical evidence and data records. Physical evidence may include computers and on-site servers, but other evidence may be gathered at a scene, such as fingerprints,

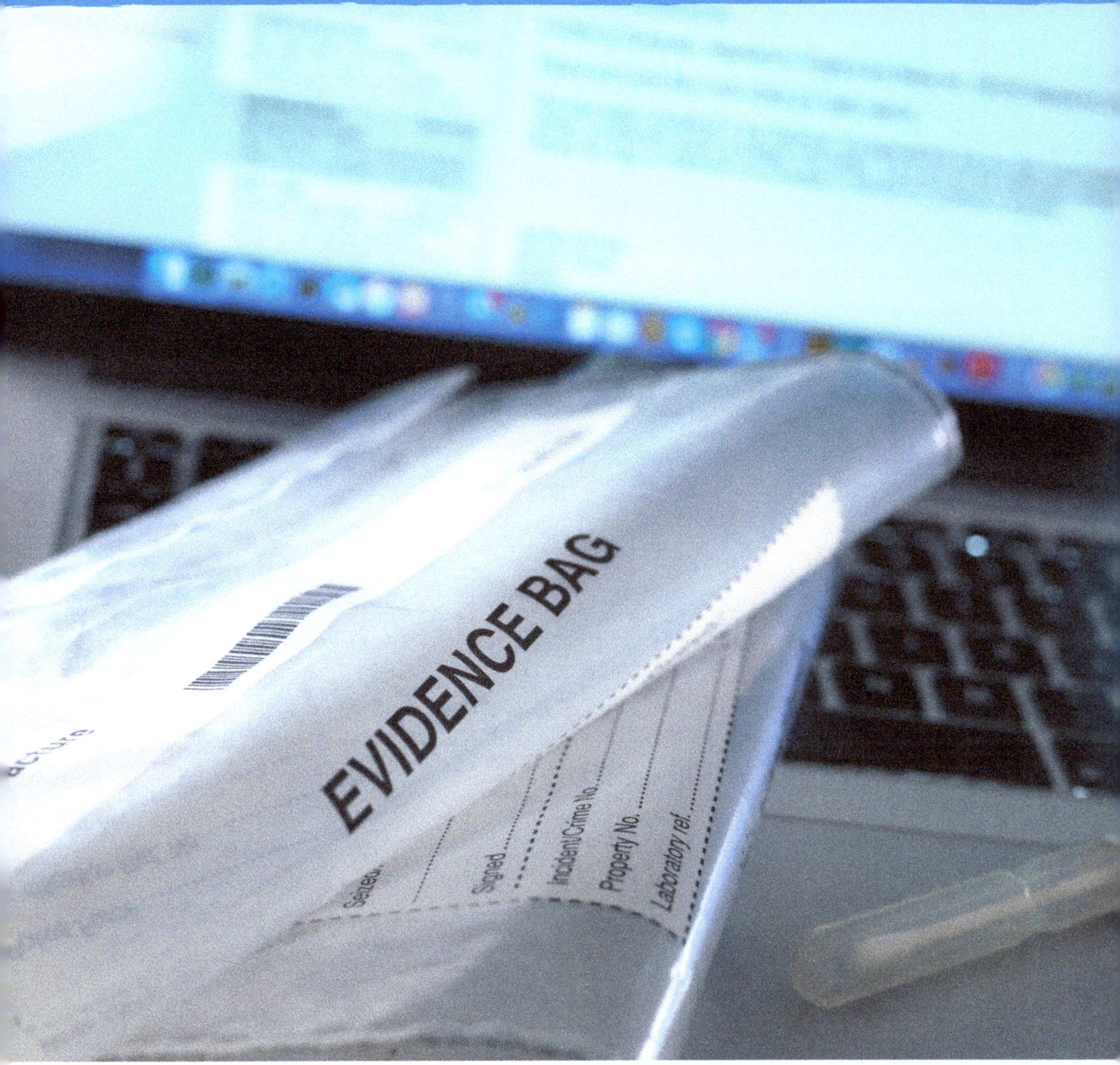

Finding, recovering, and protecting evidence are all difficult steps in the process of investigating and prosecuting a cybercriminal.

personal records, such as checkbooks and bills, and statements from witnesses. Data records may include telephone records or information from ISP servers.

Search Warrants Remain Essential

With few exceptions, the law requires that police and other government agents have probable cause to obtain a search warrant. To convince a judge that a warrant is justified, investigators need to provide specific information about the evidence they are seeking. In cases of suspected cybercrime, this includes a detailed report on the type and number of computers that they plan to search, what kinds of storage devices will be obtained, and other specifics about hardware and software. They also need to make a convincing argument that they should be allowed to seize these items.

As few police officers and attorneys are also experts in digital forensics, and some are clueless regarding computer hardware and software, law enforcement agencies will commonly have computer specialists review their warrant applications before they bring them to court. If a judge denied their request for a search warrant, there would be a harmful delay in the investigation. In addition, they want to make sure that the warrant is broad enough to include any piece of evidence that might be important to the ongoing case.

Warrants for computer crimes are unique because typical search warrants only let investigators search for a computer itself; they do not allow police and forensics specialists to search the actual files within a computer. For this reason, additional warrants are typically required for computer crimes. Such warrants allow detectives to broaden their search should they discover additional evidence of an incriminating nature. For example, a detective searching a computer for files relating to a drug case might find evidence of cyberextortion and wish to collect this evidence as well. Asking for a secondary search warrant would allow the investigator to also seize the evidence relating to the extortion.

In ordinary search warrants, police officers are required by law to clearly and openly announce their presence, typically by knocking on someone's door, before they enter private property. This is to protect suspects from inappropriate searches. However, special no-knock warrants may be obtained in some computer investigations when the case involves a potentially violent criminal or when there is a strong risk that the evidence might be destroyed. Judges who sign this type of warrant allow law enforcement to enter a private home or business without knocking or ringing the bell first so they can take the occupants by surprise. Because experienced hackers would be able to permanently destroy data on their computer if they received warning, a no-knock warrant is often the only way to protect the trail of evidence.

Digital Traps

During a cybercrime investigation, law enforcement officers expect that the suspect will have tried to delete computer evidence or encrypt it with passwords. Experienced computer forensic analysts have countermeasures for these obstacles. On some occasions, especially as technology continues to advance, cybercriminals set traps for investigators as well.

The primary reason to set a computer trap is to automatically delete, destroy, or damage any digital evidence related to someone's cybercrime. They can take many forms, but they are frequently just programs that detect when someone other than the main user is accessing a computer. This is often done by requiring the user to press certain keys or click specific desktop icons after turning the computer on. If these specific actions are not done, the trap program will start erasing the potentially incriminating files before police can access them.

By the Numbers

4.77 billion

estimated number of people who use mobile phones worldwide as of 2017

Conditions for Unwarranted Searches

In many countries, even suspects in a criminal investigation are protected from unreasonable searches and seizures of their property. In the United States, the Fourth Amendment to the U.S. Constitution guarantees this right. This is why warrants are needed. However, there are a number of exceptions to this rule. A sneak-and-peek warrant, which is allowed by the Patriot Act, permits law enforcement to search without notifying the owner—and police typically enter someone's home while it is empty. If a judge believes that a suspect's presence during the search might cause evidence tampering, endangerment to an individual, or other risks to the case, they can issue a sneak-and-peek warrant.

Investigators may also examine on-site evidence if they are given consent by another person, aside from the suspect, who shares the property. This is especially useful in the case of computers that are accessed by more than one user, whether at a home or a private business. For example, a wife or husband can permit police to search a computer used by a spouse. Parents can permit detectives to examine a child's computer, and businesses can allow employee computers to be searched without getting consent from the suspects.

Though there are a number of barriers to law enforcement when investigating cybercrime, there are also a few things that make it easier. One useful exception to standard search warrant procedure is when a network system administrator provides law enforcement with access to files on a server. According to the U.S. Department of Justice:

> *System operators have ... master keys to open any account and read any file on their systems ... System administrators typically serve as agents of "provider[s] of electronic communication service" under the Electronic Communications Privacy Act ("ECPA") ... ECPA regulates law enforcement efforts to obtain the consent of a system administrator to search an individual's account ... Accordingly, any attempt to obtain a system administrator's consent to search an account must comply with ECPA.*[28]

What this means is that system administrators are able to share or give consent for a thorough search of files that are a part of their networks. Most cybercriminals are not monitored by a system administrator, but the few that are can be easily caught if police can gain their administrator's cooperation. Still, for a majority of cybercrime cases, obtaining a traditional search warrant is the best course of action.

Experts Make Investigations

After agents or detectives obtain a warrant, they must then arrange a team of computer forensic specialists and other crime scene investigators to examine and collect the evidence on-site, as well as to interview witnesses and record images of the site. In a well-balanced investigative team, the physical search team will identify and properly mark evidence while a seizure team that carefully gathers the evidence should comprise only computer forensic experts. A sketch and photo team will record what the site looks like, and an interview and interrogation team will speak to witnesses and suspects gathered by the search team. Security and arrest teams provide on-site security, protection, and arrest support, and a case supervisor oversees the complete operation while coordinating with multiple teams and reporting progress to higher authorities, depending

Cybercrime evidence handling, whether physical or digital, can make or break a case.

Digital and Physical Evidence

To ensure that no evidence is lost or missed during a computer crime investigation, law enforcement personnel follow a set of established procedures. Presenting these procedures in court also ensures that a judge and jury will be convinced that the evidence was obtained legally and fairly, and that it is relevant to the case. While there are dozens of different exact procedures followed by the thousands of different law enforcement agencies, these are the general guidelines that could be used by any team investigating a cybercrime:

1. Locate the evidence and make a complete list of computer hardware and software seized.
2. Sort the evidence according to what is considered to be the most relevant and admissible in court and what is likely to be irrelevant.
3. Determine what is the most at-risk computer system and collect this data first. At-risk systems could be temporary file systems, online registries, portable disc drives, and caches.
4. Collect the evidence using reliable and trustworthy software tools.
5. Document, both in writing and through photographs or video, every step that is taken. Label all physical evidence and make notes about the contents and software used to collect the relevant electronic data.

on whether the case is being handled federally or locally. The investigative team, therefore, should have computer forensic experts, crime scene investigators, police officers, detectives, and an experienced manager.

Once assembled, the investigative team will require tools to carry out the on-site search. Along with the typical materials needed for any crime scene investigation, such as photography equipment, storage containers for evidence, wrenches, screwdrivers, hammers and nails, scissors and wire cutters, flashlights, and labels, the computer forensics specialists will need special electronic equipment and software.

Among the tools required for a cybercrime investigation are computer hardware and software, computer peripherals, cables, cords, power strips, surge protectors, and backup discs. Computer forensic specialists use a wide variety of software for their investigations, including imaging software, which duplicates data from a hard drive; antivirus software to protect the investigators' computers; password cracking software;

recovery and viewer software that allows detectives to locate suspect information; and text and hex editors that allow investigators to search text and image files to find relevant text and photographs, especially those that may have been altered to hide them from the police.

Handling and Preserving Evidence

When conducting on-site investigations, detectives and forensic specialists need to keep in mind several issues, including safety, integrity of evidence, and legal considerations. If they are not careful and detail-oriented, their case could get thrown out or their suspect found not guilty.

Law enforcement agents understand that even though they are investigating a computer crime, the individuals involved may be just as dangerous as suspects and perpetrators of physical crimes. They may be armed, so law enforcement will always approach with caution. Upon arrival at a crime scene, the suspects are isolated, and possibly arrested, and computers and related equipment are immediately located, identified, and guarded by an officer to prevent tampering.

When police or federal agents arrive at the scene, the first step is to record any immediately visible evidence. This includes all computers and any information displayed on their monitors, as well as any printouts easily located on desks, tables, and elsewhere. It is important to note the location of the power source for the computers and servers and to ensure that this source is not cut off, as this can result in a loss of unsaved data that could be valuable to the investigation. This also applies to other electronics, such as cell phones, music players, and even computer game systems. Any electronic device could hold a critical piece of evidence, so investigators must make sure they take care of everything.

Evidence not directly related to computers at the scene is important, too. Criminals may leave behind clues ranging from written documents to sticky notes, fingerprints, clothing, and DNA-related evidence, such as strands of hair. These must all be recorded and thoroughly documented.

By the Numbers

12,817,459

number of offender profiles contained in the National DNA Index as of March 2017

Fingerprints collected from digital devices in cybercrime investigations can reveal a lot when hardware is recovered from a potential crime scene.

Freezing Computer Evidence

Freezing the scene, a basic form of evidence collection conducted at the crime scene, is the recording of data on a seized computer. This includes any compromised and encrypted data, which is preserved using imaging software. Much of the data on a computer is saved only temporarily and is often lost when a computer is turned off, despite many auto-save features implemented on both desktop and laptop computers. Therefore, it is essential that investigators not turn off a seized computer at the scene before an investigation has been thoroughly completed. The data that should be frozen includes the files found in temporary Internet file folders, browser histories, files shared between networks and ISPs, passwords, credit card information, instant message logs, media history logs, and records of

After freezing the crime scene, investigators will typically extract all the relevant data onto external hard drives to review back at their crime lab.

recently opened files.

There are software programs that may be used by investigators to gain a quick look into the files that are saved on a computer, but the actual preservation of the data is accomplished by using imaging software. Imaging is like taking a photograph of the inside workings of a computer, allowing forensics specialists to see all the files and code exactly as the last user left them.

When files are deleted or otherwise altered on a computer, they leave behind evidence in the form of code fragments that have not been completely eliminated. If a cybercriminal has not physically destroyed a hard drive, or used a disc-wiping program that completely deletes the drive of everything, there will always be evidence of data left behind for a good forensic specialist to find.

Various software tools can be used to detect fragments of code, and it is important that the forensic specialist be careful not to accidentally alter the contents of a suspect's hard drive. The data that a computer forensics expert looks at needs to be completely identical to the data that was on the original computer. If it is not, then they could be making a false conclusion and a judge would throw the case out of court. As a result, imaging software tools are thoroughly tested before an examination of a suspect's hard drive to ensure they are functioning correctly.

Data Recovery

Because law enforcement agencies do not commonly employ full-time coders or security software developers, they rely on private corporations to make updated and reliable tools for them to use. A number of cybersecurity firms specialize in creating new software packages with forensic applications. For example, some products have a function that automatically verifies that the data on the investigator's hard drive is an exact match with the data from the suspect's computer. This is another layer of confirmation that the computer forensics expert will be able to make a valid conclusion that will be usable in court.

Another important feature that many modern forensic software programs include is the ability to check for digital traps and possibly prevent them. Because the most important tasks of officers serving a search warrant are keeping the data secure and making sure they get an exact copy, the best forensic software will automatically run checks and make sure that it notifies the users about potential hazards. Just as hackers are able to take advantage of new improvements to technology and software, law enforcement can benefit from upgrades to their investigative tools.

Breaking and Bypassing Encryptions

In addition to deleting or altering data, cybercriminals—like many other computer users—try to safeguard information by encrypting it and creating passwords to protect it. Sometimes, basic observation can help investigators locate a password, such as when a suspect has a password written on a piece of paper at the scene. If a suspect has been careless with their password, then investigators might be able to guess what it is. For example, many people use their own name or birth date, or the name of a friend, spouse, pet, or favorite musician. Detectives who already know a great deal about the suspect can sometimes guess a password without the use of password cracking software.

Because billions of people use mobile devices, smartphone encryption—and decryption—methods are at the cutting edge of technological progress.

More often, computer forensic specialists use highly specialized programs to find a password. There are a number of programs available to do this. Most programs can uncover passwords for some of the most common software programs used today, such as social media websites, e-mail accounts, and personal webpages. Passwords, however, may not only be attached to individual files or software programs, but also to the entire hard drive. A hard drive password protects the computer from being booted up by anyone who does not know the password. More expensive and sophisticated cracking tools can be extremely powerful, capable of calculating trillions of possible combinations until finding the right one. In the mid-2010s, advanced cracking software could perform these calculations within minutes.

As password cracking technology has advanced, however, so too has password encrypting technology. There are programs that can be used to encrypt password or login data to the point that it is almost impossible to break through. These programs are mostly used by average people who want to secure their personal computers, but hackers have taken advantage of the software and can use it to hide their crimes from law enforcement.

Microsoft Making Drinks

Since the 1990s, a variety of software investigative tools created have streamlined the process of computer forensics investigations. In the early days of computing, forensic investigators had to go through the labor-intensive process of searching through thousands of lines of digital code. While much of the work in a cyber investigation still involves technicians combing through data while programs search code to assist them, many of these tools can work together to extract data from a suspect's computer in a complicated—but automated—process. In 2008, Microsoft released a new, extremely powerful program to help make forensic work more efficient. Named the Computer Online Forensic Evidence Extractor (COFEE), the program is contained on a small flash drive. All an officer has to do is plug it into the computer under investigation. It instantly carries out 150 different commands to extract data without compromising the files. "It also eliminates the need to seize a computer itself, which typically involves disconnecting from a network, turning off the power and potentially losing data. Instead, the investigator can scan for evidence on site,"[29] one reporter wrote.

Law enforcement agencies in 15 countries were using COFEE as of 2008, and Microsoft has been distributing it to police and other professionals for free. The logic behind this decision is that Microsoft has a vested interest in keeping lawbreakers off the Internet and electronic devices in general, since they cater to a huge share of that market.

COFEE's security was not perfect, however, and it was leaked to several illegal download websites in 2009. Immediately, people began to worry that the powerful program, which can rapidly rip sensitive data off even secure systems, would be used by the cybercriminals it was supposed to stop. The incident even led to the announcement of a counter-program, Detect and Eliminate Computer-Acquired Forensics (DECAF) by third-party programmers. Not long after DECAF was released, the developers admitted that they created the program—which did not work—as a hoax. They wanted to draw attention to the need for global cybersecurity improvements and point out the flaws within Microsoft. Though programs related to COFEE are still used by some agencies in the 2010s, it is more often used as a hacking tool for amateur cybercriminals.

Chapter Five

Building a Case

Among the similarities of a cybercrime case to any criminal court case is that forensic specialists are trusted to determine whether the data collected supports the evidence of guilt. Computer forensics play a significant role in cases involving crimes perpetrated using sophisticated technology and, generally, the Internet. Professionally preparing the evidence in a case, accurately analyzing the data gathered, and providing testimony in court are all parts of proving a cybercrime case.

Maintaining Data Integrity

Any suspect brought in for trial as a defendant can be found not guilty if the authorities involved mishandle the evidence of the crime, so the mere presence of a potential cybercriminal in court is no guarantee of guilt. Just as with physical evidence, electronic evidence can be contaminated. Computer files can be corrupted, and this is why file backups and exact imaging are so important in investigations.

"Originals should never be used in forensic examination," explained one security expert, "verified duplicates should be used. This not only ensures that the original data remains clean, but also enables examiners to try more ... tests. Of course, any tests done should be done on a clean, isolated host machine."[30]

Good practices in collecting and labeling evidence must also be followed, just as in other traditional crime-scene investigations. Computer forensics examiners must make sure to keep a careful record of who possesses, touches, or interacts with the evidence they have collected; this is called keeping a clean chain of evidence. If someone accessed the evidence and manipulated it in some way, for example, the investigators would need to know who that person was and why they changed something. Otherwise, they could be

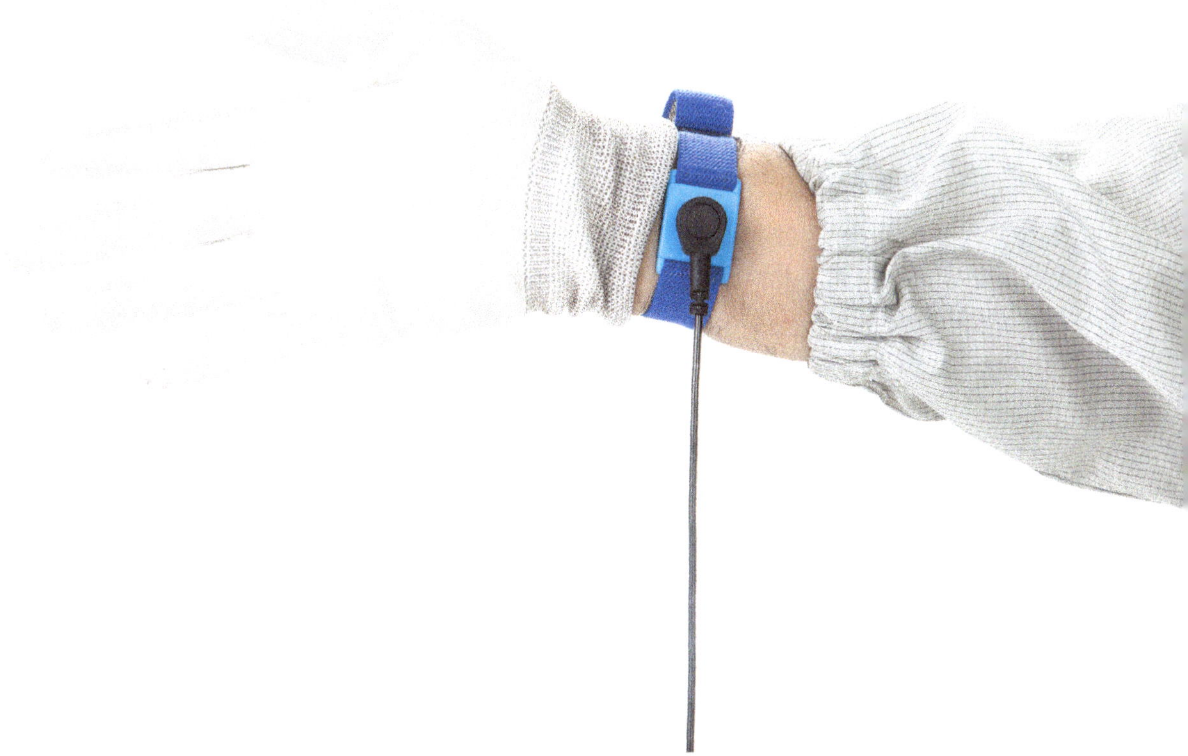

Cybercrime investigators often wear bracelets, such as the one shown here, that help make sure they do not cause electrical damage to computers.

presenting false or corrupted data to the court, which would result in having the case thrown out.

Just as with traditional crime scenes, all physical evidence at the scene of a cybercrime needs to be carefully and accurately labeled. This includes all computer components, peripherals, memory cards and discs, wires, and cables. Latex gloves should be worn to keep physical evidence, such as fingerprints, from being removed or added to the evidence. Investigators must also keep in mind that computer electronics can be damaged by dust, static electricity, overly hot temperatures, and even small magnetic fields. An inexperienced detective might not be aware of how sensitive computer material can be, so it is always critical that experts check everyone's behavior while the search is being completed.

Once everything has been properly tagged, computers and storage devices must be kept in a secure location where they will not be accessed by anyone not directly involved in the investigation and authorized to interact with them. Any access to a computer, regardless of the person's intention, by unauthorized personnel can cause data on the hard drive to be changed and make it unusable in court. With advanced software technologies, computer forensics specialists will run periodic checks on the computer that verifies that no data has been altered in any way. By keeping every link in the chain of evidence completely clean, they maximize their chances that they will be able to get a conviction.

Another issue concerning computer evidence is that data can naturally decay over time, even without any manipulation. Court cases, depending on the nature of the crime, can sometimes drag on for months or years while investigators implement software to piece together altered or corrupted data. Some storage devices, such as CD-ROMs, can begin to decay after one or two years, and older forms of memory can deteriorate even faster. Modern storage, such as external hard drives and flash drives, have assisted in delaying and, in some cases, preventing data decay, but the problem is still relevant to cybercrime cases when the integrity of evidence is called into question. Transferring data between so many memory devices can introduce some level of doubt in the mind of a judge or jury.

A Sensitive Chain of Custody

Computer files and related equipment must be documented with the same care and due process as any physical evidence. File names, document creation and modification dates, data on fragmented or partially erased files, all versions of legal and illegal software in question, the case number, and the names of law enforcement personnel handling the evidence are delicate data points which must be thoroughly documented. Keeping track of the type of software and the version is particularly important because manufacturers maintain information on known bugs in these programs that could potentially affect the data discovered.

Cybercrime evidence, including whole computers, data storage units and more, goes between many law enforcement personnel on the way to its use in a trial. Whether computer evidence travels from the scene of the crime to a crime lab and to a courtroom, it is vital to make sure that it is clear who has been in contact with the evidence along the way. Two cybercrime experts explained, "When

Getting Ready for a Jury

Court bailiffs and other members of law enforcement must follow certain procedures when preparing the data collected for the case. These procedures vary between local, state, and federal jurisdictions, but the general rules are:

1. A specific, qualified person should be assigned to monitor all the collected computer crime evidence.
2. Whenever possible, the evidence should be maintained in an untouched, unaltered state. This includes the original files, software, hardware, and any imaged or copied data.
3. If, for some reason, the evidence must be accessed and examined in a way that could potentially alter it, a competent computer forensics examiner must be present at all times, and they must extensively document everything that is done during the examination process, who is doing the examination, and why they are doing it.
4. All evidence recorded must be maintained in such a way that a third party could reproduce what was done and create the same results discovered by the original examiners. This ensures that law enforcement is not manipulating or fabricating evidence just to get a conviction.

prosecutors present evidence to a court, they must be ready to show that the thing they offer is the same thing the agents seized."[31]

To keep evidence safe and make sure it is ready for use in court, many law enforcement agencies have an evidence officer who is put in charge of recording the chain of evidence, including not only who has handled the evidence, but also whether or not anything was done to it along the way. The evidence officer also keeps notes made about tests conducted and any other comments from investigators pertaining to the evidence. When it comes time to present the evidence in court, the records kept by evidence officers can be extremely useful in persuading a judge that the chain of evidence is clean.

Evidence Analysis

In the same way there are misconceptions about many parts of the law enforcement process, raw evidence gathering is not the only task of a digital crime scene investigator—though it is a key part of the job. Computer forensics specialists analyze the data they have collected and try to make sense out of it, which includes conducting tests on computer files.

One of the many differences between a traditional investigation and a computer investigation is that it is much more difficult to trace out a series of events leading up to and around the cybercrime. Without a clear trail of data or an investigator skilled enough to decrypt the data, it would be difficult to prove anything in court. With a murder case, for instance, a detective may find evidence, such as footprints, fingerprints, blood and hair samples, and even a murder weapon, that can help establish a timeline and identify suspects. Each of these pieces of physical evidence can assist police in reconstructing what happened. With a computer, however, all that the computer

Even though computer forensics experts can do a lot for cybercrime investigations, there are limits to how much information they can learn from a suspect's computer.

forensics specialist typically has is a huge chunk of data that was found on the suspect's computer at the time that it was seized. The specialist can only theorize about the original state of the computer and about anything that may have occurred between the time the crime was committed and the time the computer was seized. Though some extremely advanced programs allow investigators to successfully recover older states of the suspect's computer, they are not widespread or totally reliable in court. One computer security expert explained why this is such a challenge:

> *If you saved every state and event of the computer ... then you could answer any digital investigation question about it. Unfortunately, a digital investigator will have only the current state of the system or the state when an acquisition was performed. Perhaps he will also have backups of the system, which represent the state of the system at a previous time. He must make [assumptions] about the previous states of the system. For example, given the current state, he must make [assumptions] about what events caused the system to get into that state.*[32]

While a computer forensics expert can figure out questions about the current state of the data on a computer, and even query about data from a past state, they cannot discover cause-and-effect relationships. For example, a computer investigator might find a file that indicates a user of the computer visited a gambling website. It is possible, however, that this information was implanted by a computer virus, or someone other than the suspect used the computer. There is no way of telling who actually input the commands, because a computer is just a machine—it is not necessarily tied to a single person.

By the Numbers

43

percentage of cyberattacks that target small businesses

Educated Guessing

Analyzing computer evidence and data is a difficult job. Since computer forensic specialists typically only have the data that was on the computer at the time it was seized to work with, their conclusions based on that data are theoretical, even with today's advances in technology. According to one expert, the most effective approach is to make educated assumptions. However, because they are just assumptions, they should not be interpreted as absolute facts.

> *We should be making hypotheses and testing them. We should be stating that we think program X was installed at time Y and test the statement by trying to prove that it was NOT installed. If we can find evidence that it was installed and we cannot show that it was not installed, then we can conclude with an amount of certainty that it was installed. However, digital forensics is not at that point yet because we have no objective way of calculating how confident we are in our conclusions. We cannot conclude that we are 80.25% confident that a file was created by a web browser (and not a backdoor trojan) because we do not [have the] data to support those types of calculations.*[33]

In many specific cases, such as proving whether a certain software program is capable of generating a specific file output, computer forensics analysts are able to answer with complete confidence. More involved processes that require a long trail of events are too imprecise and require too much data to prove in many cases. What a computer investigator can do, though, is provide an informed opinion about possible scenarios using sample data to show how a crime might have been committed.

The Daubert standard, which is a set of legal guidelines used to determine admissibility of scientific evidence in court, also commonly applies to cybercrime cases. The Wex Legal Dictionary defines the components of the Daubert standard: "(1) whether the theory or technique in question can be and has been tested; (2) whether it has been subjected to peer review and publication; (3) its known or potential error rate; (4) the existence and maintenance of standards controlling its operation; and (5) whether it has attracted widespread acceptance within a relevant scientific community."[34]

While still not a perfected science in the courtroom, analyzing digital evidence can still help investigators solve cases, convince juries, and put cybercriminals behind bars.

Data Mining: Essential to Cybercrime Investigations

Though much of the work of a cybercrime investigation still involves tireless effort in the lab, one advancement that has changed the field of analysis in recent years is forensic data mining. Through data mining, analysts extract cybercrime-related data to determine patterns and peer through large volumes of information, saving technicians and investigators a great deal of guessing. K.K. Sindhu and B.B. Meshram, two computer engineering experts, described crime data mining in four steps in a report from 2012; that report has influenced much research since.

> *1) Entity extraction [is] used to automatically identity person, login ID, password, ID [number], IP of the system and personal properties from reports or logs.*
>
> *2) Clustering techniques such as "concept space" [are] used to automatically associate different objects (such as persons, organizations, hardware systems) in crime records.*
>
> *3) Deviation detection [is] applied in fraud detection, network intrusion detection, and other crime analyses that involve tracing abnormal activities.*
>
> *4) Association rule [is] applied to finding [associations] and sequential patterns between web transactions.*[35]

Data mining algorithms are not simply used to establish patterns, but also analyze photography from crime scenes, prevent or prove evidence tampering, uncover e-mails, videos, histories, ATM logs, and much of what else an investigator needs to make a case. Data mining is not a perfect process despite how it has been particularly improved in the last few years, but it is a form of investigation many teams rely on nonetheless.

Dates and Times

With online systems functioning 24 hours a day, attacks can take place at any time—something cybercriminals use to their advantage as they operate. With hackers potentially being able to have constant access to computer grids, establishing the times when events occurred is extremely important in proving guilt in many court cases. If, for example, a prosecutor wanted to prove that a suspect was at a bank at a certain time, but a log file on the suspect's computer indicated he was writing an e-mail during that exact time, then the case could suffer a serious setback.

One might believe that establishing timelines using computers would be fairly simple because all computers include internal clocks, and file directories show when text, graphic, and other files have been saved. Most Internet pages and browsers, as well, have methods of recording exact dates and times automatically when users access them.

Computer clocks may not always be accurate, however, especially if a user has adjusted the time display; even if

Cybercriminals are known to attack vulnerabilities in the system at irregular hours, such as late at night or early in the morning.

the clock is off by only a few minutes, the difference could be significant in a trial. The internal clock on an individual computer can also be synchronized with a network clock, but then the network clock must be checked for accuracy, too. This is another instance in which data mining proves its importance, since the process can use multiple networks to establish, at the very least, a time frame depending on evidence of things such as logins.

It also should be noted which time zone the clock is set for, as it is possible

Other Dangers

Vishing, similar to phishing, takes advantage of Voice over Internet Protocols (VoIP). Like phishing, vishing uses social engineering techniques to lure people into a scam. Instead of e-mail, however, vishing uses telephone services available through the Internet, such as Skype or Discord. Most people who use this technology trust it more than e-mail because the voice communication is connected to landline telephones that are easier for phone companies to trace. However, just as with e-mails, spoofing is possible using VoIP, so it is wise to always be suspicious of anyone who is asking for credit card numbers or other personal information.

With the rise of social media, another form of manipulating people over the Internet has emerged: catfishing. This term, which takes its name from a 2010 movie and the subsequent television show, is used to describe someone who pretends to be someone else on a website such as Facebook or Twitter and takes advantage of people through those platforms. While not all catfishing is criminal, these fraudsters sometimes attempt to get personal information with which they can commit serious identity theft and continue manipulating people online. For these reasons, it is crucial to keep privacy settings on social media websites turned up and never share too much information online.

that a computer may have been moved from another time zone. Also, different operating system versions perform differently depending on their use, including the accuracy of their internal clocks. To add even more complexity to the task, the software tools that forensic specialists use also may have variations in how they record file creation and alteration times. This is why it is important that all tools used in a criminal examination be tested, and their performance documented, before their use as evidence.

Unclear Evidence

The possibility of missed or falsified evidence exists in any case, and it has greatly increased dependence on detailed investigations and reliably accurate data mining software. In computer crimes, the danger of errors can be compounded by the complex nature of computer forensics. Computer hard drives and storage devices can contain so much information—in states ranging from whole and uncorrupted to damaged, hidden, and temporary—that there are many ways data can be misinterpreted by even the most experienced forensics teams. It is also possible for criminals to create false evidence on their computers, although this is extremely difficult to do.

Some amateur computer scientists may think that all data extracted during an investigation is pure, objective fact, which is not always the case. Even when investigators have followed all the correct procedures, extracting and preserving evidence from a computer or storage device, the information on a computer is not necessarily true. All data and information needs to be interpreted and analyzed, and forensics experts are capable of making mistakes. Moreover, even though a computer can hold evidence that appears to indicate someone's guilt, they may in fact be totally innocent. As one computer expert explained, "The sources of errors in computers are wide-ranging. From computer viruses that leave [inappropriate] content in computers, to remote control via Trojan horses that allow external users to take over a computer from over the Internet, to just plain lies typed in by human beings, computers are full of wrong information."[36] That is why talented, detail-oriented computer examiners are necessary.

Providing Expert Testimony

Even today, a troublesome aspect of computer evidence is that, in many circumstances, it is considered hearsay by the courts. Hearsay evidence is information that is not based on a witness's personal knowledge. In other words, a witness cannot testify about something they heard someone else say—that information is considered unreliable. When a computer forensics specialist testifies in court about evidence found within a computer, the computer, in the eyes of the law, is the real "witness." Some leeway is granted in courts for this, and it makes the reliability of the expert on the stand all the more important. It is vital that the testimony comes from a source that is experienced, talented, and capable of explaining everything they are testifying about.

Beyond hearsay, another difficulty with evidence in a cybercrime investigation is that the sciences of data mining and image enhancing, while advanced, have margins of error just like any other technology. Often the error is small and many juries believe that the data can still be considered valid beyond a reasonable doubt. Even these fractional error percentages are subject to some debate, however, and defense attorneys can use their imprecise nature to persuade a jury of innocence. Moreover, this room for error introduces the issue of absolute proof to cybercrime, which has been a problem in the realm of physical evidence gathering for hundreds of years.

Technology Continues to Advance

The tools to combat cybercrime are most often the same tools used to perpetrate it, and keeping ahead of the criminals is a constant challenge for law enforcement. A big concern is that the

Internet has become a massive database of information about how to hack into computer networks and commit other cybercrimes, all without the need for sophisticated technical knowledge. Those who wish to perform attacks on individual computers or networks need only find the right malware package, download it, and run it, allowing them to automatically perform multiple operations that could only be accomplished by knowledgeable programmers in the early days of computing.

Search engines such as Google also have become unwitting tools of cybercriminals, who have figured out how to conduct Internet searches to locate websites that use outdated or

In the 2010s, innovation started to branch into wearable technology, such as smartwatches. The more things that connect to the Internet, however, the greater the threat of cyberattack.

Popular Culture

As technology evolves, books, television shows, and movies feature science fiction (sci-fi) themes that are becoming more popular than ever. This is partially because most sci-fi imagines a future with dramatically advanced forms of technology and communication. The reality is that these stories often depict innovations that are not drastically different concepts from those already proposed and widely anticipated—or feared.

The popular sci-fi show *Black Mirror* is one example. Each episode of the show is an hour-long look into dark reflections of social trends as humankind moves toward more technology. It is particularly popular for touching on modern trends, such as discrimination, digital social interaction, and dependence on technology. One episode of this series, "Shut Up and Dance," depicts a teenager falling into an online cyberextortion trap much like those that really exist today: The cybercriminals access private computer cameras, cellphones, and other devices remotely, with little to no trouble breaking encryptions, and record embarrassing videos of their victims. The episode also discusses the morality of these criminals as online vigilantes and the privacy of individual Internet users.

vulnerable software and exploit those weaknesses. Furthermore, the IoT is causing more everyday items—from watches to refrigerators to dog collars—to connect to wireless Internet networks. Some of these advances, including cloud networks and other services, have helped business run smoother and added convenience to billions of people's lives. However, the risk of cybercrime is only increasing alongside the rise of technology.

Digital Protection

Even though cybersecurity has become a major government priority, the first line of defense against cyberattacks is often private citizens and corporations. People who do not use firewalls, antivirus software, or other defenses have suffered greatly at the hands of hackers, crackers, and other black hats. Recently, two of the major computer hardware providers, Microsoft and Apple, have come to recognize that it is in their best interest to provide better security for their customers. Apple's new operating systems set strong examples of how modern companies design software to include security—and security updates. Smaller, competing operating systems, such as Linux, have also emerged, promising even fewer security threats than Windows or Mac OS. Some networks themselves, such as college Wi-Fi networks, require virus protection before allowing people to access it with computers or mobile devices. Many universities even offer free programs to protect their students.

Since the mid-2000s, major software developers have been coming up with new and secure ways of storing online data. These sometimes take the form of specific applications, such as Windows Defender, that are in place in all computers running that operating system. Specific browsers, such as Google Chrome and Mozilla Firefox, also have security extensions that an average user can easily install on their own. There are dozens of reliable, reputable antivirus software programs available online, and some are completely free. Though no software package is completely perfect, these can go a long way in protecting personal information from cyberattack.

One of the broadest misconceptions regarding cybersecurity is the difference between Macintosh (Mac) and Windows (PC) operating systems. As the two biggest competitors in the computing world, there has been a lot of marketing and advertisement in support of both brands. One claim that has gained immense popularity is that Macs are more secure than PCs; many people make this argument because fewer Mac users experience harmful viruses. However, PC users are quick to point out that there are far fewer Mac users globally, which means hackers are only focused on writing programs to attack PCs. While both Mac OS and Windows have seen substantial improvements with each new version and upgrade, the fact remains that neither is totally safe. No one should think they are completely protected from cybercrime—even the government or the largest corporations in the world. It is always important to install additional software to keep digital files secure.

Since the fields of computer forensics and cybercrime advance at nearly the same rate, there is no doubt that this form of crime will remain one of the focal points of law enforcement in the future. As long as the technological tools remain available to the mass market, the same tools developed to protect people are bound to be put to criminal use. Cybercrime has emerged as, arguably, the most prevalent threat to global, national, and personal security in the 21st century, and just as it is the responsibility of authorities to stop these kinds of criminals, it is also their responsibility to learn from them. Though security advances often come after the damage, computer crime investigators can only hope to encourage and contribute to the development of new technology as often as possible.

Notes

Chapter One: Defining Cybercrime

1. "U.S. Army Commercial: 'Cyber'" YouTube video, 0:31, posted by GOARMY.COM, October 24, 2016. www.youtube.com/watch?v=0LZnOorfS_Q.
2. David S. Wall, *Cybercrime: The Transformation of Crime in the Information Age*. Cambridge, UK: Polity, 2007, p. 49.
3. Wall, *Cybercrime*, p. 50.
4. Wall, *Cybercrime*, p. 50.
5. *Computer Security Handbook*, Seymour Bosworth, M.E. Kabay, Eric Whyne, eds., 5th edition (Hoboken, NJ: John Wiley & Sons, 2009) s.v. "Equity Funding Fraud (1964–1973)."
6. Serge Krasavin, "What is Cyber-terrorism?," Computer Crime Research Center, accessed May 24, 2017. www.crime-research.org/library/Cyber-terrorism.htm.
7. William L. Tafoya. "Cyber Terror," FBI Law Enforcement Bulletin, November 2011, accessed May 24, 2017. leb.fbi.gov/2011/november/cyber-terror.
8. "Incidents of Ransomware on the Rise: Protect Yourself and Your Organization," FBI News, April 29, 2016, accessed May 24, 2017. www.fbi.gov/news/stories/incidents-of-ransomware-on-the-rise.
9. Scott J. Bernazzoli, "Sextortion Affecting Thousands of U.S. Childrem," FBI News, April 4, 2016, accessed May 24, 2017. www.fbi.gov/contact-us/field-offices/pittsburgh/news/press-releases/sextortion-affecting-thousands-of-u.s.-children.
10. Wall, *Cybercrime*, p. 17.
11. Steve Morgan, "Cyber Crime Costs Projected To Reach $2 Trillion by 2019," *Forbes*, January 17, 2016, accessed May 24, 2017. www.forbes.com/sites/stevemorgan/2016/01/17/cyber-crime-costs-projected-to-reach-2-trillion-by-2019/#6683aea43a91.
12. Morgan, "Cyber Crime."

Chapter Two: The Internet as a Crime Scene

13. Carl J. Franklin, *The Investigator's Guide to Computer Crime*. Springfield, IL: Charles C. Thomas, 2006, p. 73.
14. Matt Richtel, "In the Pursuit of Cybercriminals, Real Detectives Rely on Amateurs," *New York Times*, May 17, 2000, accessed

May 24, 2017. www.nytimes.com/2000/05/17/business/in-the-pursuit-of-cybercriminals-real-detectives-rely-on-amateurs.html
15. Robert Lemos, "Hackers Look to Hide Communications," CNET, August 1, 2003, accessed May 24, 2017. www.cnet.com/uk/news/hackers-look-to-hide-communications/
16. Jose Pagliery. "FBI Hackers Took Down a Child Porn Ring," CNN, January 25, 2016, accessed May 24, 2017. money.cnn.com/2016/01/25/technology/fbi-child-porn/
17. Jason Walker, telephone interview by the editor of *Cybercrime: Using Computers as Weapons*, May 11, 2017.
18. Eoghan Casey, *Digital Evidence and Computer Crime: Forensic Science, Computers and the Internet*. Waltham, MA: Academic Press, 2011, p. 29.
19. Casey, *Digital Evidence and Computer Crime*, p. 31.
20. Franklin, *Investigator's Guide to Computer Crime*, pp. 181–182.
21. Franklin, *Investigator's Guide to Computer Crime*, pp. 185–186.

Chapter Three: Tracking the Suspects

22. Bradley Mitchell, "What Is a Network Sniffer?," Lifewire, October 12, 2016, accessed May 24, 2017. www.lifewire.com/definition-of-sniffer-817996.
23. John R. Vacca, *Guide to Wireless Network Security*. Pomeroy, OH: Springer, 2006, p. 582.
24. Tim Cook, "A Message to Our Customers," Apple, February 16, 2016, accessed May 24, 2017. www.apple.com/customer-letter/.
25. Quoted in C-SAIT, "honeynet project," C-SAIT, accessed May 24, 2017. www.sait.fsu.edu/research/honey/index.shtml.
26. Mark Jewell, "Study: Many Retailers' Wireless Data Systems Easy to Hack," ABC News, accessed May 15, 2017. abcnews.go.com/Business/story?id=3872929&page=1
27. Margaret Rouse, """Wi-Fi Protected Access (WPA)," TechTarget, accessed May 24, 2017. searchmobilecomputing.techtarget.com/definition/Wi-Fi-Protected-Access.

Chapter Four: Evidence Is Everything

28. Bruce Middleton, *Cyber Crime Investigator's Field Guide*. Boca Raton, FL: Auerbach, 2002, p. 183.
29. Benjamin J. Romano, "Microsoft Device Helps Police Pluck Evidence from Cyberscene of Crime," *Seattle Times*, April 29, 2008, accessed May 24, 2017. old.seattletimes.com/html/microsoft/2004379751_msftlaw29.html.

Chapter Five: Building a Case

30. Matthew Braid, "Collecting Electronic Evidence After a System Compromise," SANS Institute, accessed May 16, 2017. www.giac.org/paper/gsec/659/collecting-electronic-evidence-system-compromise/101519.
31. Peter Stephenson, *Investigating Computer-Related Crime: A Handbook for Corporate Investigators*. Boca Raton, FL: CRC Press, 2000, p. 133.
32. Brian D. Carrier, "A Brief Introduction to the Computer History Model," Digital Evidence, accessed May 16, 2017. www.digital-evidence.org/hist_model1.html.
33. Brian D. Carrier, "A Brief Introduction to the Computer History Model."
34. *Wex Legal Dictionary* s.v. "Daubert Standard," accessed May 16, 2017. www.law.cornell.edu/wex/daubert_standard.
35. B.B. Meshram and K.K. Sindhu, "Digital Forensics and Cyber Crime Data Mining," *Engineering Science and Technology: An International Journal* 2, no. 1 (2012), accessed May 16, 2017. www.estij.org/papers/vol2no12012/19vol2no1.pdf.
36. Fred Cohen, "Challenges to Digital Forensic Evidence," in *Forensic Computer Crime Investigation*, Thomas A. Johnson, ed. Boca Raton, FL: Taylor & Francis, 2005, p. 177.

For More Information

Books

Gray, Judy Silverstein and Taylor Baldwin Kiland. *Cyber Technology: Using Computers to Fight Terrorism*. New York, NY: Enslow, 2017.
Focused on the broader scale of massive cyberattacks that have an impact on the security of a nation, this book explains how dangerous the modern Internet can be.

Hayden, Michael V. *Playing to the Edge: American Intelligence in the Age of Terror*. New York, NY: Penguin Press, 2016.
This book chronicles two decades of U.S. intelligence from the perspective of the author, a former director of the NSA and CIA.

Perdew, Laura and Sherali Zeadally. *Online Identity*. Minneapolis, MN: Essential Library, 2017.
This work is focused on the benefits—and dangers—of storing personal information online.

Timmons, Angie and Sara L. Latta. *Investigating Cybercrime*. New York, NY: Enslow, 2018.
Giving the reader some perspective on what it is like to fight against cybercrime, this book also includes specific and detailed explanations of the many different kinds of digital lawbreaking.

Waschke, Marvin. *Personal Cybersecurity: How to Avoid and Recover from Cybercrime*. Bellingham, WA: Apress, 2017.
Included in this book are tips, tricks, and advice for maintaining a high level of computer safety, with information that can apply to both personal life and business operations.

Yount, Lisa, ed. *Does the Internet Increase the Risk of Crime?* Detroit, MI: Greenhaven Press, 2006.
This book offers opposing viewpoints about how and whether the development of the Internet has led to more crime in society.

Websites

"A Brief History of Cyber Crime"
(www.floridatechonline.com/blog/information-technology/a-brief-history-of-cyber-crime)
Discussing some of the biggest cybercrime cases in the history of computing, this website also has links to further reading on cybersecurity and technological advice.

Computer Crime and Intellectual Property Sections (CCIPS)
(www.justice.gov/criminal-ccips)
This is a U.S. government website that provides an overview of federal law enforcement, news articles about cases involving cybercrime, and primary-source documents.

Cyber Crime
(www.fbi.gov/investigate/cyber)
Hosted by the FBI, this website has brief, informative explanations of the different forms and functions of a variety of online criminal activity.

Cybersecurity
(www.dhs.gov/topic/cybersecurity)
This official website, run by the United States government, has a broad overview of cybercrime in addition to more detailed explanations of how experts help protect the Internet.

"Ransomware Attack Reveals Bitcoin as an Accessory to Cybercrime"
(www.cbc.ca/news/business/ransomware-bitcoin-threat-cyberattack-1.4115344)
This detailed article discusses the consequences of 2017's massive global ransomware attack, and debates whether anonymous online currencies are dangerous.

Index

Photo Credits

Cover Benoit Daoust/Shutterstock.com; p. 7 photokup/Shutterstock.com; p. 8 Bruce Rolff/Shutterstock.com; p. 11 Speedkingz/Shutterstock.com; p. 13 NurPhoto/Contributor/NurPhoto/Getty Images; pp. 14, 16 Rawpixel.com/Shutterstock.com; p. 19 Alexey Boldin/Shutterstock.com; pp. 20, 40, 54, 89 Bloomberg/Contributor/Bloomberg/Getty Images; p. 24 DANIEL LEAL-OLIVAS/Stringer/AFP/Getty Images; p. 29 Mark Van Scyoc/Shutterstock.com; p. 30 Carsten Reisinger/Shutterstock.com; p. 33 Glow Images, Inc/Glow/Getty Images; p. 35 STEPHEN JAFFE/Staff/AFP/Getty Images; p. 41 Rob Bouwman/Shutterstock.com; p. 43 South_agency/E+/Getty Images; p. 48 rvlsoft/Shutterstock.com; p. 50 Bettmann/Contributor/Bettmann/Getty Images; p. 52 360b/Shutterstock.com; p. 56 David M G/Shutterstock.com; p. 59 Wutlufaipy/Shutterstock.com; p. 61 Aimee M Lee/Shutterstock.com; p. 65 Andrew Brookes/Cultura/Getty Images; p. 69 Mike Theiler/Stringer/Getty Images News/Getty Images; p. 72 Steve Heap/Shutterstock.com; p. 73 dourleak/Shutterstock.com; p. 75 oatawa/Shutterstock.com; p. 79 Suthisa/Shutterstock.com; p. 82 AP Photo/Manuel Balce Ceneta; p. 86 emeravideo/Shutterstock.com.

About the Author

Michael E. Sciandra graduated from SUNY Purchase in 2015 with a double major in Creative Writing and Journalism, with concentrations in fiction and poetry as well as hard news and literary journalism. Growing up in Buffalo, New York, Sciandra has published for various online and print magazines in the metro area and Nevada, formerly the Sports Editor for the *Lahontan Valley News*. He is now continuing to pursue his passion in poetry while embracing freelance work for Lucent Books and other firms.